Business for Pleasure

By Anthony Johnson

Business for Pleasure
By Anthony Johnson
All Rights Reserved

This book is a work of fiction. Names, characters, places and incidents are products of the author's imagination, or are used fictitiously. Any resemblance to actual events or locales or persons, living or dead is entirely coincidental.

Published by Anthony Johnson
Cover design by Anthony Johnson
Cover Illustration by Jerome Brown
Rose picture-http2.bp.blogspt.com
Author's photo by Anthony Johnson Jr.
Proofing by Kimberly Hill
Edited by Tonya Greene

ISBN-13:978-0-615-68469-7

Dedication

In Loving Memory of my belated wife Yolanda L. Johnson. Thank you for my beautiful son Anthony Jr,. and for all the lasting memories we will continue to share of you.

Ingrid H. Johnson, and all those whom have gone on before us; we pray that you rest in peace always.

As a man, I am a true believer in the power of love. When a man loves a woman there's nothing you can do to keep him away from her. Love is silly, love is strong, and love is the melody of that beautiful song.

Whether you yearn to find this thing called love, or if you already have it, its berries shall quench your every thirst. Trust that your love is real. Protect it from harm, and always find the strength to fight for it.

You are about to experience the most unconventional way to say I love you. You will witness one woman's focus, and one man's journey to be next to the woman of his dreams. She is his one, his vice, and his everything!

Thank You,

Anthony Johnson

Acknowledgements

----Thank you father GOD for your unwavering grace and mercy, and thank you for your one and only son Jesus Christ.

---To my son, Anthony Jr., You are my drive, inspiration, and purpose in life. For you, I give my all. You are the best son any father could ever dream of having. The time that we spend together warms my heart like nothing else. It makes me so proud to watch you grow into such a respectful and intelligent young man. You make me happy when I'm sad. You provide light where there's darkness. Everything I do is to ensure your happiness, security, and quality of life. I will continue to live my life in a way that I may be a positive role model for you. I'm glad you're my son. I'm very proud of you, and I love you.

---To my father, Raymond Sr., for always supporting me no matter what, and for showing me what a man is. Your strength has taught me to never give up. Your shoulders have taught me that I can bear any load.

---To my mother, Ramona (Granny), GOD was pleased with me when he chose you to be my mother. Thank you for all you do for us. You have been my biggest support system of all. Anthony Jr. and I are so grateful for all that you do to help make our transitions more comfortable. We are so blessed to have you here with us to enjoy our lives with. I pray that GOD continues to bless you as the woman of GOD that you are.

---To my siblings: LaTonya, Raymond Jr., Lenardo (Scooby), and Al, for always believing and supporting me, and for all the crap you all put up with from me. You guys are the best group of brothers and sister that any person could want. I wish upon the world at least half of the fun that I've had living my life with you four nuts.

---To the rest of my family, friends, and loved ones; I say thank you for being who you are to me. Thank you for always showing me love and support. You each know who you are, and that is with the highest admiration. I love you all.

---To my attorney and great friend Mr. Phillip Ransom, you are the best legal representation anyone could ask for. Thanks for 20 years of dotting my "I's" and crossing my "T's."

---To the world's greatest editor, Ms. Tonya Greene. Thank you for the knowledge, patience, and insight that you brought to this book. Thanks for pushing and encouraging me to give my readers more. You have truly made a difference with this work. Thank you.

--- To my Bishop, Edward M. Clark, and my church family at Live Oak Baptist Church of College Park, Ga; I would like to extend a special thank you. My spiritual grounding is what allows me to move freely through a world of uncertainty. Thank you Live Oak for twenty-three years of membership, "YOU WILL KNOW US BY OUR LOVE."

Editor's Note

It was a pleasure to work with platinum song writer, Anthony "Teno" Johnson. After hearing of his success with the writing of **Freak Me**, by Silk, I knew his new urban romance novel would be a must read. **Business for Pleasure** is an emotional love story that captures its readers from the very beginning. It continues to hold them in suspense until the end of the novel. By bringing its readers to tears, anger, and laughter; this romance novel unveils true love at its finest. Johnson continues to dazzle the mind with his new release.

Tonya Greene, MA. Ed, author, editor, *Why Does A Woman Need A Man, Sweet Whispers into My Spirit, and Angels From Above*

Table of Contents

Chapter One

"In the Beginning"

I t was August 20, 1999 in College Park, GA. The halls of M.D. Collins High School had everyone running around in total excitement because it was the first day of school. There were students everywhere! Some met for the first time. Some were old friends and discussed their summer breaks. Of course everyone else simply checked out each others' new school clothes. One kid in particular stayed to himself. He never bothered anyone or got much attention because he was pretty quiet and reserved. As he walked through the hall trying to anxiously find his way to class-BAM! He was overturned by some older upper classman who was escorted by his entourage. As he got up from the floor, the upper classman grabbed him by the neck of his new school shirt, ripping his shirt in the process.

He slammed the young man up against the wall and said, "The next time you see me coming, you better move to the other side of the hall. The next time you get in my way, I'm gonna beat the shit out of you and send you home to your momma crying!"

Petrified the young man just stared at the upper classman, almost in agreement. It was at that moment things went from bad to worse. It was worse, not for the young man being bullied, but most certainly for the upper classman. Out of nowhere someone jacked up the bully and slammed him face first into the very same wall that he slammed the young man into. He was then turned around and commenced to get the hell beat out of him. He was punched, slapped, and kicked. You name it, and he got it. The friends that he had with him, that knocked the young student down ran like the cowards they were.

After whipping up on the bully, the person who stepped in defense of the young student looked around at all of the spectators and asked, "Who else wanna fuck with lil' man?"

Everyone turned and went on their way. Someone called EMS, and the upper classman was taken to the hospital in an ambulance. No one was brave enough to say who beat old boy's ass. Therefore, the defender was never suspended or expelled because of it. The person that came to the young man's rescue looked down and asked him, "You alright lil' man?"

"Yeah," the young student replied. "Thanks for coming to my defense," he added.

"It's cool," the hero replied. "What's your name lil' man," he asked.

"Kendall...Kendall Jackson," the youngster replied.

The defender then looked at the young student and introduced himself, "I'm Rolex."

No one knew his real name. Besides, he was not one to question about anything. Rolex grew up in College Park, GA. He lived the kind of life that most parents spend their lives making sure that their children don't have to live. Coming from a single parent household, his mother, Ms. Jackie, was responsible for raising him. However, being an alcoholic made that extremely hard to do. Rolex took to the streets, or should I say he took the streets over. To call him a total social misfit would be putting it lightly.

"I live next door to you in Biscayne Apartments," said Rolex.

"Yeah that's right!" Kendall exclaimed. "I be seeing you outside smoking weed with your partners! Look like ya'll be smoking some of that Bill Clinton chronic," joked Kendall as his personality shined through his forgotten fear. Kendall was the smart, very silly, but street smart guy.

Rolex started laughing. "You kind of cool lil' man. I'm going to call you K.K... Look, you can tell everybody you my little brother."

"Ok!" said K.K.

"Meet me in the parking lot after school. You can ride home with me," said Rolex.

"Alright," said K.K.

"I got to get to class," said Rolex. They both headed in the direction of their classes. Just as they started to walk off, two female students walked past. Their names were Cecilia and Monét. Cecilia looked at Rolex and rolled her eyes. When Cecilia walked past Rolex, the ice grill that she was giving, melted him like a piece of chocolate in the Georgia sun. Rolex just stared at Cecilia as if he were in a trance. He snapped out long enough to say, "Don't roll your eyes baby, let me carry your books and take you to the game on Friday."

Cecilia rolled her eyes a second time and smacked her teeth. With rejection on her lips replied, "Whatever," as she continued on her way to class.

K.K., who had witnessed the whole scene looked at Rolex and said, "DAMN man! You looked like E.T. just rode across your momma's grass on that ugly ass bike!"

Rolex cracked up laughing and then he added," She is so fly. Imma get her one day." They both laughed and went to class.

As the years progressed, K.K. and Rolex became tight like brothers. They spent much of their time hanging out and partying together. Rolex took to K.K. because he was different from the other guys on the block. He wasn't in the streets. Rolex looked out for K.K. and made sure that no one messed with him...EVER!

K.K. was raised by his mother, Ms. Jackson, a nurse. She worked nights at Grady Memorial Hospital. Hanging around K.K. and Ms. Jackson gave Rolex an escape from his lifestyle. K.K. and Ms. Jackson went to church every Sunday. Rolex would be invited every week, but always declined. These guys were as close as brothers. It hurt K.K. when the hustle moved Rolex away from College Park.

Rolex perfected the drug game, stolen car business, and ran a successful bootleg operation. He continued this life of illegal enterprise for years before turning it in for a life of illegal and black market gun sales. It's been said that Rolex was one of the biggest movers of fire arms this side of Mississippi. Rolex made over $20 million in the life before getting out. Some say he should've been dead a long time ago. K.K.'s urging was one of the main reasons Rolex got out of the game.

One day Rolex received word of a tragedy, Ms. Jackson had passed way. Rolex rushed to K.K.'s side. K.K. told Rolex that he didn't want to bury him next. Then he started to talk to him about the Lord. Rolex opened up to Christ.

Rolex stepped up as a true friend to K.K. when his mother Ms. Jackson died. The death of K.K.'s mother almost destroyed K.K. He didn't know what to do or where to go. It was just him and his mother. Without his mom, K.K. was lost. Rolex convinced K.K. to see a counselor. Rolex felt a counselor could offer enough help for K.K. so that he could start the healing process. At first K.K. rejected the idea. Through continued suggesting, Rolex was able to convince him to go. K.K. went to the counselor on a regular basis for about a year. In one year's time, he started living again and healing. This is what his mother would have wanted.

When Rolex came back to Georgia for K.K.'s mother's funeral, he was rich and doing well. With all that, you would think that he would be happy, but he wasn't happy.

K.K. told him, "You have everything a man could want: women, fast cars, huge cribs, and money! You're unhappy because you're tired of the life! Not tired of your life. You want to enjoy life more now. You're getting older and simple things are starting to matter to you man. I think it's time for you to give it up Bro. You don't have the passion for it anymore. You're just good at it."

Rolex fought K.K. on it, but he didn't ignore him. He told K.K. that at the time, the game was something he had to do.

"Everybody always knew of the battle my mother had with alcohol. My mom had a friend

Ms. Betty, and when I tell you she was a lush, I mean it. She either had something to drink in her hand, was going to get something to drink, or she had just finished her drink before you walked up. That was Ms. Betty, and we loved her anyway. One night, it all changed for that family. Everything went wrong." With a dead stare on Rolex's face, he dug deep inside his soul to tell of this story.

"One night Ms. Betty's son Jerry came home from hanging out with some of his partners. It was about 3 o'clock in the morning. The lights in their apartment were on so he figured his mom had company or something. Jerry decided he'd just speak and head on up stairs for bed. Upon opening the front door to the apartment, he witnessed an image that would haunt any 19 year old boy for the rest of his life. When he opened the door he saw this fucking junkie standing over his mom beating the shit out of her over some drugs they had been doing that night. He never had a clue that his mom was fucking around with dope. He grabbed that junkie and beat his ass out into the street. There, he continued to beat him into the black asphalt. He then stuck that junkie in his trunk and drove off. They found that junkie tied to a tree in the woods about three weeks later with 17 bullets in him. It's sad because Jerry was a real good friend of mine. He's doing 25 to life for the murder. I'm sure he's not proud of what he did that night. At that time all he could probably think about was that man beating his mom. So he did what he felt he had to do to protect her."

"Hustling was what I felt I needed to do to make it out of the hood K.K.," Rolex confessed.

"Yeah, Rolex, I get you, but you out now. Your time for hustling needs to be over." urged K.K.

K.K. started taking Rolex to church with him introducing him to his Bishop and some of his friends at the church. The bond that Rolex gained with the fellows, and hearing of their testimonies, made Rolex think more about getting out of the game.

"K.K. to be honest with you, I had been thinking about getting out of the game for a while. Yes, the money, and the underworld fame had always kept me in it. Man, but those exact things are what turn that world against you. The amount of money that I had coming in made me a target for a lot of people. I could tell they were going to come after me. I started laying low. I changed my habits up some. I switched up the cars I drove, tinted all my windows, and changed my wardrobe. They still came after me K.K. They came to get me man!"

Very emotional, body shaking, and fist clenched Rolex began to tell of the day he was to be murdered.

"I was chilling at my crib in Miami. I had some of my partners over to watch the game that day. Everything was cool K.K., but then I heard it man! I knew what was happening. They came through the windows on us man! When we heard the glass breaking, we all started grabbing our straps. It was too late! They started flipping my whole house with AK's and 12 gauges. They shot everybody man!" With tears running down his face, Rolex continued to tell of this horrific slaughter inside of his home.

"They killed everybody. I was the only person that survived it. The doctors still don't understand how I made it out alive." Rolex stood up in front Of K.K. He lifted up his shirt and revealed a mangled surgically reconstructed tarsal. "They took out half of my colon, and a piece of my stomach to save my life man. The police said my girl was the last to die. They said she was tortured and died at the hospital that night. She told the police that the hit men told her that it was too bad they were there, because I was the only one they wanted. I went away for some time after that K.K. That's why you didn't hear from me for that length of time two years ago. Revenge was the only thing on my mind during that time. When I finally hit Miami again, I went with a crew of motherfuckers that mattered. After we got done, I didn't have to watch my back any more. I left Miami for good. I have to admit that going to church, fellowshipping with the brothers at the church, and fellowship with the rest of the congregation has really put me in a good place with GOD."

Eventually, Rolex actually started to open up to the word of God. About one year later, Rolex officially got out of the game and turned his life over to Christ. He later started his real estate development company, and has been living his life legit and for Christ ever since.

Now Rolex lives a very private and legit life. He used his money to become a very powerful real estate investor and developer. Years later, Rolex even gave K.K. a job as Site Manager over all of his real estate projects, with his real estate development company. Rolex and K.K. even attend the same church, The Oak Baptist Church as adults in College Park, Ga. Over the years they have really been a help to each other. He attributes all of his success to Jesus Christ because today, Rolex is a Christian man. Serious about his walk with Christ, Rolex's focus is on living for GOD.

Chapter 2

"A Pleasant Surprise"

I t was a warm, slightly breezy Saturday afternoon and K.K. decided that he would take this time to go run some errands.

"I'm about to leave out Homie. Do you want me to do anything for you while I'm out," yelled K.K.

"No, I'm alright," Rolex replied.

With that, K.K. was on his way. He let the top down to soak up some of Georgia's sunshine. K.K. ran all around town. He paid bills, picked up dry cleaning, and handled some business at the post office. After about three hours had passed and the errands were completed, K.K. decided to head back home.

On his way back home, K.K. remembered that he wanted to stop by the local record store to pick up some music. Upon arriving to the store, he saw a crowd of people. Curious as to what was going on, he proceeded into the store to find that there was an autograph signing for a male vocalist in progress.

As K.K. navigated his way through the throngs of fans, he saw a seemingly powerful woman directing every aspect of the event. Any questions asked by the staff were directed to her. Any and all commands that were given came from her. It was quite obvious that she was in control. What was even more noticeable about this powerful woman was the angelic beauty that poured over her like warm honey.

Stuck like a deer in headlights, K.K. stood mesmerized. Drawing her into his vision, something began to look familiar to him. He was unsure of what it was. As he stared, he struggled to understand what it was about this woman. Then like a ton of bricks, it hit him! "Cecilia," he whispered softly to himself, as if trying to avoid disturbing a sleeping baby. It was at that exact moment that he and Cecilia Bajon locked eyes. Focused like a hunter's scope, she smiled, and nodded her head. Then motioned with her finger that he should approach the VIP section where she was sitting.

Strong, beautiful, smart, ambitious; all these words describe this focused, driven, and successful black woman from the hood. Born and raised in the city of College Park, GA, Cecilia was the only child to Cynthia and Joseph Bajon.

Raised strictly to focus on education and her Christianity, Cecilia did just that. A great student throughout her entire educational career, Cecilia graduated high school with honors. She went on to accept a four-year academic scholarship at a HBCU; Spellman College. She completed her schooling and received a degree in marketing. Cecilia moved away from Georgia to pursue her career after graduation.

Growing up in the hood, Cecilia made countless amounts of friends and associates. She also had a lot of male admirers growing up. Her parents never accepted her having boyfriends. There were some guys that she liked and couldn't date. Then there were others who she didn't like and never even gave them the time of day. Yet and still, they all loved her.

Mutually excited about seeing each other after so many years, K.K. and Cecilia hugged and greeted one another. Their conversation was brief because she was working and had to maintain her focus on the task at hand. Cecilia gave K.K. her business card and told him to keep in touch.

They quickly said good bye and solidified their happiness about seeing each other with another hug. After picking up the CDs that he had come to the store to get, K.K. left the record store excited to have run into Cecilia. K.K. looked back for one more glimpse, hopped in his ride, and drove off.

Driving frantically, K.K. had one destination in mind, home! K.K. sped, ignored the traffic signals, ran stop signs, and even cut a few drivers off. It was only luck that he didn't cause an accident, or hurt anyone in the process. Finally, with his subdivision in sight, K.K. raced down a few streets before reaching the driveway to his residence. He jumped out of the vehicle, barely giving himself time to turn the engine off. K.K. ran up the elegant concrete steps that lead to entry way of the lavish home he shares with Rolex. K.K. hit the front door like a runaway bus.

"Rolex! Rolex!," shouts K.K.

A startled Rolex ran into the living room to see what all of the commotion was about. He found K.K. out of breath and anxious.

"Calm down,"Rolex shouted. "What's wrong?" he demanded.

"Nothing's wrong. Man you'll never believe who I just saw," K.K. exclaimed.

"Who?...Tell me who," said Rolex.

"Cecilia Bajon!"

Cecilia Bajon was the Director of Product Management for a major record label. She was responsible for artist development with the label. From the album to videos; Cecilia was in charge of the Label's product. She was a woman very committed to her career. She was so committed in fact, that she never even made the time for marriage or children. Now living back in Georgia, she resided in Buckhead. This was an affluent part of town just north of Atlanta. Buckhead was also conveniently located close to the record label's office. Cecilia has by her own choice, decided to stay away from dating. Instead, she opts to spend time with her aging parents who still live in College Park where she grew up.

Cecilia and her mother still shared a very close relationship. One of their favorite things to do was to sit in the kitchen laughing and talking over a snack, and something to drink. While the ladies talked it up in the kitchen, Cecilia's dad usually remained glued to the television in the living room.

Rolex always thought about Cecilia. He's always had a crush on her. In high school, no one besides K.K. ever knew about Rolex's feelings for Cecilia. Rolex revealed it to him on their ride home one day after school. There were a few times back then that he spoke to her, but she never responded. Due to his lifestyle and bad reputation she wrote him off as trouble. Rolex kept that crush close to him, only speaking of her once in a while, and then only to K.K. He figured he couldn't have a girl like Cecilia. For that reason he chose not to pursue her at that time.

After hearing this news, it might as well have been Christmas morning at the Macy's parade and he wouldn't have known it. The stare in his eyes was that of a dying man in mid-fall before hitting the ground.

"Rolex! Rolex! Rolex," K.K. shouted. "Man what the hell is wrong with you? You got gas or something?"

"Man I blanked out when you said her name," replied Rolex. "I'm ok though."

"What's wrong? Why you trippin," asked K.K.

Rolex, in a very somber tone replied, "I did what I had to do."

"Man what are you talking about," K.K. replied.

Rolex looked at K.K., told him to sit down and said "Man let me talk to you."

True to form K.K. started in with the comedy. "Man this some gay shit aint it? Please tell me this ain't no gay shit. Rolex you been looking at me man?"

"Shut up!" Rolex shouts, "Now listen…… Back when we were in high school, I always wanted that woman. I knew I didn't have a chance because of the life I lived. I always felt I could have had a shot if I wasn't in the game. I couldn't give it up. I had to take care of myself and my mom. I didn't feel like I had a choice. I felt I was doing what I had to do. That's all it was. There comes a time in life where you can't necessarily see the repercussions for the chance itself. Man, I used to have thoughts of giving it all up and going back to the old hood to find her. I never wanted anything that didn't benefit me financially. Making money has always been my life's goal. I never knew love like some people get the chance to. My own mother was drunk all the time when I was growing up. My days consisted of making sure she made it home safely, and hustling so we wouldn't get evicted from our apartment. Now, I'm not asking for sympathy votes or anything, but I just feel like Cecilia would've responded to me differently had I not been in the game. Life brings about things that make you stop and take notice. Cecilia is that for me. It didn't matter where I was, what I was doing, or who I was with, I would stop instantly the moment I saw her. I would watch her walk by until she vanished from my sight. Every time I saw her I swore that if I had a chance to be with her, that I would love her more than I love myself." Rolex spoke thoughtfully.

"Well what you need to do is get in touch with Cecilia and see what's up with her. She didn't have a ring on, and she was looking like a damn swimsuit model! I was about to scoop her ass up because you know she was checking a brother out and everything...." coaxed K.K.

"Whatever," Rolex replied, as he snatched Cecilia's business card out of K.K.'s hand. "You think she'll take my call," asked Rolex.

"Hell naw," replied K.K.

"You think she'll respond to my e-mail?" Rolex tried again.

"Hell naw," exclaimed K.K.

"Well then why are you telling me to holla at her," Rolex asked.

"Because you be looking like a sick ass puppy with fleas on his balls whenever you talk about her. I be feeling sorry for your ass man," said K.K.

"Well I'm just going to go by her job and see her," said Rolex.

"Man I hope you ain't got no warrants because she might call the police as soon as she sees your ass," K.K. joked.

Rolex playfully jumped in K.K.'s face causing him to retreat.

"Naw man, I'm just saying, the last time she saw your ass you were robbing handicapped people for their parking permits," joked K.K.

"I'm going," Rolex declared.

"That's cool. Just leave some bond money on the table just in case!" K.K. shouted back to Rolex' as he walked toward the door.

When he arrived at the door, Rolex turned around and said, "Very funny, but I don't think that'll be necessary. The only money that I will need to spend will be on a very beautiful and romantic dinner when I take Cecilia out!"

Anthony Johnson
Business for Pleasure

Chapter 3

"When Yesterday Meets Today"

The very next week Rolex prepared himself to do the hardest thing that he has ever done. He was as nervous as a deer during hunting season. He went through about 10 suits, 5 different colognes, 6 watches, and 5 different pairs of shoes trying to find the right combination to make a good impression on Cecilia. His progress was interrupted as K.K. knocked on the door to his bedroom.

"Man what you doing? Are you auditioning for the Apollo or going to see Cecilia," he asked.

"Man I just want to make the right impression. First impressions are everything," Rolex replied.

K.K. stared in disbelief. "You mean to tell me a drug dealing, boot-legging, illegal arms dealer about to pop up unannounced on a Christian executive woman whose idea of a good time is probably talking to her girlfriend during every commercial break while watching American Idol, is worried about what color suit to wear? Man please!"

"Alright man, you're right," Rolex agreed as he proceeded to get dressed and head over to the record company. All the while he was hoping that Cecilia would be there.

As he arrived at the lobby of Spineum Entertainment Group, Rolex was greeted by an attractive receptionist.

"Welcome to Spineum Entertainment, May I help you," she asked.

The way she looked at Rolex said that she wanted to help him with more than just the original purpose of his visit.

Rolex kept his focus. "Yes, I am here to see Cecilia Bajon."

"Do you have an appointment," The curious receptionist pried. She was wondering what business this handsome stranger had with Cecilia.

"Ah no, I don't have an appointment. I'm an old friend paying a surprise visit," replied Rolex.

The receptionist, able to sense Rolex's uneasiness, figured that he had more invested in this visit than he was letting on. She raised one eyebrow.

"Ok. Please have a seat in the waiting area. I will let her know that she has a guest.

You may help yourself to coffee or tea while you wait," she suggested.

Rolex thanked her and headed over to make himself a cup of tea. He picked up a cup from the table and filled it with hot water. He opened the pouch that held the TAZO tea bag. As he slowly dipped it in and out of the water, his thoughts raced a million miles per hour.

"Am I making the biggest mistake of my life," Rolex asked himself. "Should I just walk out now since she doesn't know who is out here waiting for her? Maybe it would be better, he reasoned, that way I can still hold on to the possibilities..." He convinced himself that if he left the building all of the fantasies that he had over the years about how things would be if they were to ever run into each other at this point of their lives would remain intact. He could still hold on to the hope that maybe, all things considered, she would want him now. Rolex truly felt that if this visit went wrong, that it would crush him. He couldn't bear to lose the possibility of making Cecilia the woman of his life.

Despite the discouraging thoughts that entered Rolex' mind, honestly speaking, a herd of wild cattle couldn't have drug Rolex out of that office building. Just knowing that he was about to be face to face with the woman that he secretly desired for the past fifteen years evoked a feeling in Rolex that he couldn't even describe. Trying desperately to calm his emotions and pull himself together, Rolex sat down and sipped his tea. As he turned his attention back to the receptionist, he heard her dial Cecilia's extension.

A voice came over the speaker and said, "Yes Kelly."

"You have a guest in the waiting room Ms. Bajon," the receptionist replied. She locked eyes with Rolex. "He doesn't have an appointment. He says that he is an old friend dropping in to surprise you."

Thinking that it was most likely K.K. waiting for her in the reception area, Cecilia agreed to see him.

"You can send him in," she replied.

"Sir, you can go in now," the receptionist gestured towards Rolex. "Ms. Bajon's office is the corner office at the end of the hall on the left."

"Thank you very much." Rolex smiled as he looked down the hall that the receptionist was directing him to. The hallway that lead to Cecilia's office seemed to stretch at least a mile long. Rolex took a deep breath, and took his first steps toward the woman he had been thinking about for the past decade or more. Every step was calculated, like stepping from rock to rock on a rushing stream. He noticed every picture that hung on the walls. Carefully, he read each name tag on every door. Finally, he reached the corner office at the end of the hall on the left. His eyes were glued to the brass name plate on the door. It read: *Cecilia Bajon, Director of Product Management.*

Rolex's mind flashed back to 1986. He was 7 years old. He was standing in front of the Sunday morning congregation at church wearing a suit that was too hot, and a bow tie that was so tight he could barely breathe. Rolex stood petrified. He had to give a solo performance with the children's choir at his Grandmother's church. When Rolex's mind came back to the present, there he stood in that long hallway, which evoked the same emotions he'd experienced as a seven year old in front of the church. From out of nowhere he heard K.K.'s voice in his head, "Man what the hell you doing? Knock on the damn door!"

Instantly, Rolex gained his composure, collected his thoughts, and did what he had came to do. He raised the beautiful bouquet of long-stemmed yellow roses chest high. He raised his hand, and ever so gently, but with confidence knocked on the door. A few seconds passed, and the door knob turned in what seemed like slow motion. The door slowly opened. Confirmation of God's perfection was revealed. There stood Cecilia Bajon!

Very confidently Rolex spoke, "Hello Cecilia. Long time no see."

Without saying a word, she looked at the man who stood before her as though she were admiring a brand new Mercedes Benz, still parked on the showroom floor. She noticed his perfectly lined hair cut and trimmed mustache. The width of his shoulders was perfectly encased in his tailor-made Italian suit. The Rolex timepiece on his wrist was pregnant with diamonds. His size 13 shoes were pure alligator.

"Please come in," Cecilia said from behind the only partially opened door. The confused look on her face told Rolex that he'd better be quick in stating the purpose of his visit.

"I don't mean to be rude," Cecilia spoke. "But can you please refresh my memory?"

"Yes Cecilia," Rolex replied "Growing up you knew me as Rolex."

Unable to register where she knew or had heard that name before, Cecilia's mind was in deep thought. Her eyes left Rolex and drifted down to the floor. An empty stare registered on her face. Memories started to flood Cecilia's mind reminding her who the man standing before her was. Her eyes widened and then without delay her confusion turned to horror!

"What do you want with me?" She spoke in a very direct, afraid, nervous, yet curious tone.

"I don't want anything from you. I just wanted to see you. I wanted to see how life has been treating you, that's all," said Rolex.

"Why do you care how life has been treating me? Rolex, why am I even on your mind? How did you find me? What's really going on here? We have no past! Rolex why are you here?"

"You're right Cecilia, we don't have a past. That is one of the things in my life that I've always regretted," Rolex spoke candidly.

"Ok!" Cecilia spoke with indifference laced with venom. "Is this visit supposed to heal those wounds or make some kind of difference?"

"Well, I was hoping that I might be able to sit down and talk to you. You know the type of life I lived back then. I just want to show you what a changed man looks like," Rolex explained.

"A changed man you say," Cecilia questioned him with a raised eyebrow.

Before Rolex could respond, Cecilia lit into Rolex like he was a criminal and she was the prosecutor. "Ok, let me tell you what this changed man looks like to me...like somebody that will get me a felony possession charge when I am riding in your car. You get pulled over and they find something illegal. I could get my head blown off, or raped by some drug dealers that are trying to send you a message. How about the $400,000 condo I just bought get seized when the Feds start thinking that your dope money purchased it. Oh, oh, let's not forget how you'll come home and beat the shit out of me every time a deal goes bad...NO!" She shook her head and continued on, "The only thing you can show me Mr. Rolex is how a changed man looks walking out of my office!"

Rolex laid the roses on Cecilia's beautiful cherry wood desk, stood up, and said, "I deserve that. Thank you for your time Cecilia."

With that, Rolex turned to walk out of Cecilia's office. As he reached the door, he heard Cecilia call his name. Thinking that maybe she had a change of heart, Rolex quickly turned around.

"Yes," he replied. His hope was apparent in his voice.

Cecilia preceded to hand him the flowers that he brought her. "Take these. I don't want to feel like I owe you anything," she scoffed.

Defeated, Rolex took the flowers and left. Feeling nothing but regret for having showed up at Cecilia's office, Rolex exited the building.

The more he thought about the decision he made to go see Cecilia, the more he started to feel better. In some strange way, Rolex started to feel a sense of happiness in the fact that he finally got the opportunity to see Cecilia despite the outcome. All he could think about was how beautiful she was and how good she smelled. Rolex was happy as well as disappointed.

When Rolex returned home later that evening, he was still taken by the response he received from Cecilia during his surprise visit. How do you come to grips with saying goodbye to someone you never had? How do you stop dreaming? How do you turn what if into never mind? The truth of the matter is, there is no way. You just heal. You just try to make it. You just focus on other things. You just find that inner person inside of you, and talk to him. Whatever you do....don't talk to K.K.

"Damn! She shut you down like that?" K.K. interrupted Rolex's thoughts. "Man that shit gotta hurt! Did she cut her eyes at you like

Claire Huxtable? Did she call security? Tell me what happened," he demanded.

Rolex took his time in responding. "Today I grew. I stood in the presence of the woman I've thought of for over 15 years. She was more beautiful than I could have imagined. She commands the space she is in. She spoke so eloquently. Her smile took me on a journey. I was moved by the class that exuded from her. The scent of her perfume filled the room and seemed to purify the air. This woman did not receive my visit as I would have wanted her to, but I experienced her today. What I gained will last me another ten years. So I guess I will say it didn't go good. It went great!"

"Man, what the hell kind of bipolar shit is that," said K.K. "You just got cursed out, kicked out, beat down, flowers thrown back in your face, and heart ground up like hamburger meat. She's probably down town putting in a restraining order against you for stalking. All that and you're up in here acting like Holyfield when Benny Hinn told him that he could fight! What's really going on?"

Rolex shook his head and chuckled at K.K.'s exaggerated recap of the day's events. "I went, and I gave it a shot," Rolex replied. "No hard feelings. You win some, you lose some. That's all to it." Rolex shrugged his shoulders, walked over to the couch, sat down, and stared at the fire rumbling in the fireplace.

"Man are you in denial," K.K. asked.

Rolex looked up from his trance. "Let it go K.K., just let it go."

As Rolex returned to his inner thoughts he knew that he was going to have to find some way to channel all these feelings he was experiencing since seeing Cecilia. *I think I will start writing.* Rolex thought to himself. Rolex retired to the private quarters of his beautiful Atlanta mansion, where he would sort out his feelings of the day's disappointments. He stretched out over a leather wing back lounging chair, located in the reading area of his master suite.

He spun the tip of a hand rolled Cuban cigar over the flame of a 14k gold lighter, as he sipped on a glass of Dom Perignon. The room was filled with the sounds of soft jazz playing in the background. The mood was calm, mellow, and specific to how Rolex was feeling that lonely evening.

Rolex began to think about Cecilia's beautiful hair, and how it flowed down her back. He thought about the tone of her voice and how she spoke to him earlier that day. It was bitter sweet he thought, but he accepted the good with the bad.

Rolex decided that night to leave the details of his future in the hands of GOD. Rolex relied on his new found faith in Christ that night. As his head hung back and his eyes closed, he made a vow.

Part of his vow was to always care for Cecilia. He understood that her feelings toward him were based on past knowledge of the man he used to be. The other part of his vow was to never stop trying.

Rolex began to write just as he said. He wrote poetry about love, lust, loss, friendship, pain, misery, hope, and beauty. Of course, they all led back to one person, Cecilia. His poems became more defined as he wrote. He produced some of the most beautiful expressions of love that one could imagine. Rolex became comfortable with believing that he and Cecilia would probably never be a couple. That did not stop him from fantasizing about the possibility of what they could be. He wrote when he was happy, sad, and discouraged. He wrote all of the time. Writing had pretty much became Rolex's way of coping with life. He poured his heart and soul into the hundreds of pages that filled up with words from his heart. He never wanted to share his writings with anyone. Only he knew how much joy and pain they expressed. A man's journey can never be totally understood by another. Therefore, Rolex never wanted to explain his feelings to anyone again as it pertained to Cecilia. He simply continued to write...

Anthony Johnson
Business for Pleasure

Chapter 4

"When love walks your way"

Six months had passed since Rolex and Cecilia's meeting. One day, while browsing at Lennox Mall K.K. spotted a familiar face in the crowd. It was Monét, a girl that he and Rolex went to school with. When she spotted K.K., she also recognized him immediately. They smiled and began to make their way towards each other. She was standing about 5'4" and 120 lbs with smooth brown skin, long and pretty hair. Monét was a vision of beauty to K.K. They hugged and exchanged their hellos. When they ended their embrace K.K. asked, "So, what's been going on in your life since high school?"

Monét proceeded to tell K.K. about how she went to cosmetology school after graduation. "I own my own beauty salon in Buckhead. I have a son named Gerod. He is six years old. I'm no longer with my son's father."

"Why?" K.K. cut right to the chase. He couldn't imagine a man being stupid enough to leave this beautiful, intelligent, and successful woman alone to fend for herself and their child.

"Well, he's not as responsible as I need him to be for me and my son. I can't count on him to meet me halfway in raising our son. You know the drill. He makes promises he doesn't keep, and he can't keep a stable job. He doesn't provide any type of financial support. So there you have it! That is what I have been up to for the past few years. What about you," Monét asked as she smiled at K.K.

"First of all," K.K. responded, "I want to say congratulations on your salon and for being a mom. I'm sure you're a great mother!" K.K. wanted to let her know that he really did commend her efforts in business and parenthood before he told her what he'd been up to for the past few years. "I work for a real estate development company as a site manager. I don't have any children yet. I would like to have them someday though. My hobbies include flirting with beautiful beauticians at Lennox Mall." K.K. and Monét both fell out laughing.

During his conversation with Monét, K.K. happened to mention that just six months earlier he had run into Cecilia at an album signing. Much to K.K.'s surprise he learned that Cecilia and Monét were actually still as close as they were in high school, and Monét had been styling Cecilia's hair for years.

"She mentioned to me that she saw you at one of her artist's signings."

"Cool," replied K.K. "I didn't know you all were still close."

"Oh yeah," Monét replied. "She is just trying to figure out what she's going to do about her job."

This revelation made K.K. raise an eyebrow and ask, "What do you mean?"

"The artist she was working with, well, his project flopped. She didn't get the bonus she was expecting. The label told her that if she doesn't get them a hit act, they're going to have to let her go," explained Monét.

K.K. made Monét feel so comfortable. She didn't realize until after the fact that she had just blurted out her best friend's business. In an awkward moment, she and K.K. both just stood there. She bit her lip, not knowing where to take the conversation from there.

"Damn! Who she work for? Big Red," K.K. joked, lightening the mood.

Monét had to laugh at that one. "I can keep you laughing baby, if you let me contact you," K.K. flirted.

Monét pulled out one of her business cards and handed it to K.K. "Yeah, you can call me sometimes," her eyes flirted right back with K.K.

K.K. took the card from her and asked, "Now, when you say to call you sometimes, do you mean like it was good to see you, or call me if you hear about a class reunion or something.....or are you feeling me and want to hear from me within the next couple days?" K.K. continued to joke.

"Boy give me a call at the shop tomorrow. You so silly!" She giggled.

"Alright then, that's what I'm talking about," said K.K.

They hugged one more time as they said their goodbyes. As they both headed off in different directions Monét looked back to catch K.K. looking at her butt.

K.K. was busted! He tried to play it off. "What? I thought you said something."

"Yeah right!" She playfully rolled her eyes, trying not to make it so obvious that she was blushing. She turned around and went on her way.

Later that evening while hanging out with Rolex, K.K. mentioned bumping into Monét at the mall.

Rolex, do you remember Monét who went to school with us," asked K.K.

"Yeah," replied Rolex. "She was kind of short and real cute, right?"

"Yeah," K.K. responded. "I ran into her at the mall today. Man that girl is so fly! I hollered at her for a minute. She's doing hair now. She told me that she owns her own shop in Buck head."

"So, did you at least get her number?" Rolex inquired.

"Of course," K.K. said with an air of cockiness. "Imma call her ass too! I was tripping because she is actually good friends with Cecilia."

"Really," exclaimed Rolex, losing his composure for a quick second.

"Yes," K.K. answered. "She was also telling me that Cecilia is in a pretty bad situation at work."

"What kind of situation," Rolex interrupted before K.K. could finish explaining.

"Monét was telling me that Cecilia's job is in jeopardy. The artist that she was responsible for did not do well in record sales. Because Cecilia was the head of their project, she didn't get the bonus she was supposed to receive from the sales." K.K. continued on without even taking a breath. "Monét also told me that the label has informed Cecilia that if she does not bring a hit artist to the record company, she'll be fired! Ain't that some fucked up shit?"

"Damn," Rolex spat. "I sure hate to hear some craziness like that. Cecilia doesn't deserve that! I am sure she gave them all she could. It's not her fault they didn't sell. How could it be her fault? I don't get it!" Rolex thought out loud as he paced the floor.

"Man, I don't get it either," K.K. interjected. "I wish her all the best, but in the meantime, I'm gonna holler at her girl Monét and see what's cracking,'" K.K. said as he walked backwards out of the room leaving Rolex alone with his thoughts of Cecilia.

Rolex hated that Cecilia was having problems and he was not able to immediately reach out and rescue her. Rolex thought long and hard to find a solution to Cecilia's problem. He kept coming up with nothing. He had to face the fact that there was nothing he could do to help the situation. For a man with the unlimited resources that Rolex had, that was a very difficult pill to swallow.

"K.K.," Rolex called out, hoping that he could catch him before he left the house.

"Yo! What up?" K.K. came strolling down the stairs and back to the den where he had left Rolex.

"You think it would be a good idea to help Cecilia out with some money," Rolex asked.

"Yeah, money always helps," K.K. replied.

"What about $50,000?" Rolex put a dollar amount out there causing K.K. jump out of his seat.

"Man you can't just be giving people $50,000! Are you crazy? That girl ain't gonna take that kind of money, especially not from you!" K.K. tried to talk some sense into his friend.

Frustrated to no end, Rolex threw his hands up and said, "Well how can we help her then? It's not like we have a hit artist to give her."

It was at that very moment that it came to K.K. He jumped around in excitement like Ed McMahon just walked up to his door and presented him with one of those big ass fake checks from Publisher's Clearinghouse.

"Man that's it," he yelled.

"What's it?" Rolex was baffled.

"Give her a hit artist," K.K. explained.

Rolex looked doubtful. "And just how do you suppose we do that?"

"My boy Teno does music. That cat is dope! He has artists over there. You could put the money up to do a hit album on one of his artists and take the act over to Cecilia's label. As long as they're under Cecilia, she will get credit for the artists' success. She will get her bonus and her job would be secured. It's perfect." K.K. had it all planned out. "There's only one thing," he added.

"What's that," Rolex inquired.

"She can't know you're behind the artist," K.K. answered.

"Why is that?" Rolex was puzzled.

"Negro! She gave you back your flowers, kicked your ass out of her office, and probably went and bought a pistol," K.K. reasoned.

Rolex walked back over to his spot on the couch, sat down slowly and rubbed his chin. "Yeah, you right, it'll probably be best to keep my name quiet." He continued "Set up a meeting with Teno here at the house so we can plan how everything needs to go down."

"Alright man," K.K. replied.

A week later Teno showed up at Rolex's house for the meeting. "How are you doing," asked Rolex.

"Everything's good" he replied.

"I have a writing and producing team. We specialize in in-house production situations like this one," said Teno.

"Since K.K. has explained to you what we are doing here, tell me, based on your professional experience, what direction should we move in," asked Rolex.

Teno spoke at this time. "I feel since the industry is booming with solo artists right now, it may be a good time to come up with a strong R&B/POP solo artist with a heavy street vibe for radio. Trust me, they'll love it," Teno interjected. "I was also informed of the importance of keeping your name confidential. That won't be a problem. For publishing purposes we can use K.K.'s real name as the administrator for publishing and mechanical royalties."

"Great!" Rolex liked the idea. "I was wondering something. I've been writing poetry ever since the last time I saw her. Most of my poetry is about her and a lot of it is what I would say to her if I ever had the chance. How realistic is it to put some of this poetry to music," Rolex asked.

"Putting your words to music is a wonderful idea. That is how songs are made, by placing lyrics to music," explained Teno. "What we will do is, put together a hot track with a platinum hook, then we'll use your poetry for the verses of the songs."

"As a matter of fact, we can do every song on the album like that," Teno added. "That way, you can have the conversation you wanted to have at her office through this album. You'll finally get the chance to say everything you feel."

Teno had Rolex sold. "Sounds like a plan. Where do we start?" he asked.

"With a check," Teno replied, everyone laughed.

"I'll do the album for $100,000 and we should have it done in about 3 months," Teno said, steering the conversation back to the business at hand.

Teno chose the best solo artist they had on their roster, a guy named Vybe. Teno immediately busied himself with putting together the tracks and hooks for the album project. They did ten songs total. Three weeks into production Teno brought Rolex into the studio along with Vybe for the purpose of customizing each song. When production and all vocals were complete, Teno flew to NY to mix down and master the album.

With street heavy hot tracks and hooks, the melodic vocal stylings of Vybe, not to mention the beautiful words penned by Rolex to Cecilia, they had a platinum award winning Grammy status album on their hands for sure! At the completion of 3 months, twelve weeks to be exact, Teno presented Rolex with the masters for the album. Rolex's plan was set in motion.

Anthony Johnson
Business for Pleasure

Chapter 5

"The Master Plan"

K.

K. studied the card in his hand as he listened to the phone ringing on the other end.

> Spineum Entertainment Group LLC.
> Cecilia Bajon – Director, Product Management.
> cbajon@spineum.net
> 777-9311

"I *sure hope this plan works for that dude. Rolex won't rest until he knows that Cecilia Bajon is taken care of,*" thought K.K.

A sexy professional female voice interrupted his thoughts, "Cecilia Bajon is speaking."

"Hey this is K.K.. What's going on Cecilia?"

"Oh not too much, just keeping with industry changes, that's all. What's up with you K.K.," Cecilia responded.

"Well the way I saw you handling your business with that music thing, I thought of you first when my partner let me hear this new R&B/POP artist that he just did a full album on," said K.K.

"Oh really?" K.K. had piqued Cecilia's curiosity.

"Yeah this guy is so off the chain it is ridiculous," knowingly reeling Cecilia in with his words.

"You wouldn't happen to be looking for any new acts would you," he asked.

"As a matter of fact I am," Cecilia replied. K.K. had her full attention.

"Well why don't we set something up? I can bring him and the producer up to the label so that you can hear him for yourself," K.K. said.

"That sounds like a winner," Cecilia replied as she scrolled through her electronic calendar. "Why don't we schedule an appointment for next Monday at 10:00am?"

"That'll work," K.K. responded.

"I really appreciate you keeping me in mind K.K. This could be bigger for me than you can imagine. Thank you so much K.K. "If there is anything I can do for you let me know."

K.K. didn't miss a beat. "Yeah there is something you can do for me. Tell your girl Monét that you think I'm fine, and that she'd be crazy not to holler at me!"

Cecilia cracked up laughing.

"What," K.K. asked. "He He Hell! I'm dead serious girl."

"Ok, ok silly, I'll talk to her for you. I'll see you guys on Monday and thanks again."

As soon as they hung up the phone K.K. immediately began to contact everyone involved in the project to inform them of the day and time that he and Cecilia had agreed on for the meeting. Cecilia too started placing the necessary calls. Her first call was to her A&R director and then to the V.P. She wanted to tell them about the prospects. Everyone was fired up and ready to go. The plan was coming together.

Later that night when Cecilia was at home relaxing, she called her girl Monét to tell her all about the opportunity that K.K. presented to her earlier that day. She was excited about the possibility that this solo artist could really be her get out of jail free card, so to speak. Her enthusiasm was not lost on Monét.

"Girl calm down I can barely understand what you are saying," Monét joked. "I'm just kidding, you should be excited, and I am praying this thing works out for you."

"Thank you girl," Cecilia said. "I know all this excitement may seem a bit premature, but for some reason when I was talking to K.K. earlier today I just felt like I could take him at his word when he said that this artist was off the chain. I hope he knows not to come at me with no broke-down-wanna-be singers." They laughed.

"Speaking of K.K., he had a message for you." Cecilia told Monét what K.K. said about her. They couldn't help but to crack up at his silliness. Monét mentioned that she and K.K. had been spending time together. She was really starting to like K.K. Cecilia couldn't help but to be happy for her friend.

"Monét you really deserve someone nice, someone that will treat you right, care for you, and make you smile. K.K. seems like a really good guy, and I am happy for you."

"Aww thanks Cee. It means a lot to hear you say that. Now let me get off of this phone and start dinner," Monét said.

"Ok girl, talk to you later." They ended their conversation.

On the other side of town K.K. and Rolex sat in Rolex's living room and rehashed the plan. They impressed themselves with their brilliance. If the plan unfolded the way they imagined it would, this thing would blow them up!

"Man what if this album really goes platinum, double platinum, or triple even," Rolex asked.

"Then I'm rich dude, that's what," K.K. stated as a matter of fact. "Now I know you ain't about to run all this publishing money through me and not leave some of it with me? Plus, it was my idea!"

"I know all that," Rolex interrupted. "You'll be well taken care of," he assured.

K.K. stood up, folded his arms in front of him and inquired, "When you say well taken care of, do you mean I'll have enough money where I don't have to steal your change when you ask me to make a run for you? Or do you mean well taken care of where I don't have ask you for shit?"

Rolex shook his head "You straight man, chill."

"Naw, but seriously man, if you just ride this thing on out, you can really show her just how much you have her best interest in mind. You have to let it play all the way through before you make it known that you are the one behind all of this," K.K. said seriously.

"Oh yeah, I will let things happen. I really like this whole thing. It allows me to help her, do things for her, build up her bank account, and let her experience money as I know it; whether she's with me or not." Rolex had a faraway look in his eye as he thought about Cecilia. "I can sit back and watch her smile, watch her bask in her success, and become one of the most sought after women in the business. That woman has done it by herself for her whole life with no man to protect and support her. I could be that man for her. I can show her what it means to be in a loving relationship, and that "Real Men" do exist. Chivalry is not dead!" Rolex's words were heavy with conviction.

"Man you ain't about to sit up here and cry are you," K.K. asked. "I mean you sound like you just got out of jail and you trying to talk some chick out of her panties! That was some real sensitive, vulnerable shit you were saying.

I'm uncomfortable talking about that ole touchy feely shit with dudes. To be honest man, I'm scared cause you bigger than me and I don't know no karate!" K.K. dodged the throw pillow that Rolex threw at his head. They both cracked up laughing!

K.K. met up with Teno the next evening. They called for a dance and performance rehearsal for the entire weekend. K.K. had the solo artist Vybe going over his show over and over again, until all the kinks were ironed out. It was very important that he looked like a polished professional. For that reason; K.K. and Teno kept a very critical eye on him during rehearsals.

"These people are not going to invest hundreds of thousands of dollars, even millions of dollars into an amateur," Teno spoke to his artist. "You must be poised, exciting to watch, and a joy to listen to. If you can offer these things, then, and only then will you get the record deal," he added.

The two men tied up some last minute business as they sat and watched the solo artist rehearse for a few more minutes. Vybe was feeling anxious about the meeting, but it was set. All he could do was show up with his A-game. Confident that Vybe had his routine locked down, K.K. rose from his seat, slapped dap with Teno, and prepared to leave.

"I'm up outta here. I'll see you guys on Monday...good luck," wished K.K. With that he walked out of the door and made his way to Monét 's house for the evening.

Monday morning at 10:00 a.m. sharp as K.K., Teno, Cecilia, and Vybe sat around the table with the label execs the tension in the room was so thick you could cut it with a knife. Every piece of furniture in the room looked high-tech. From the wall that automatically opened up to reveal an 80" video screen, to the state of the art audio system with its huge Bose speakers. The huge mahogany conference table they sat around had a finish on it that made it appear as though it were made of glass. Around the table were the softest leather recliners. Cecilia started the meeting by introducing everyone around the table. She then proceeded to grab a remote control from the caddy that sat on the table in front of her. As she pointed it in the direction of the audio system, she said, "Without further adieu, I present to you Vybe," as she pressed the play button.

Every song that played was a hit with the executives. It was obvious that they were feeling the album by the way they were moving and dancing in their seats. The signing of this solo artist was a done deal. The Label offered a full eight album recording contract. Everyone was happy, especially Cecilia. She once again could rest, knowing her position with The Label was secure. K.K. and Teno shook hands with the executives, and let them know that their attorney would reach out to them soon to discuss the details and solidify the deal. Words of congratulations could be heard all around the room. The mission was accomplished.

As soon as he was outside of the doors of the building that housed the label, K.K. phoned Rolex to deliver the good news. "They want to sign," he exclaimed, as soon as Rolex answered the phone.

"Yes!" Rolex's enthusiasm matched K.K.'s.

K.K. went on to explain how the meeting went, careful not to leave out any details about how Cecilia and the other executives were vibing to the music. Immediately after he and K.K. ended their conversation, Rolex called Phil Ransom, his attorney. Rolex gave Phil the full rundown of events, from his and K.K.'s plan, all the way down to the meeting that had transpired earlier that day. He told him everything that K.K. had told him. Phil couldn't help but laugh at Rolex and K.K.'s antics, but business was business, therefore he wasted no time contacting the label. After nearly three weeks of negotiations, reviewing clause after clause, loophole after loophole, the two parties were able to reach an agreement, and seal the deal.

Cecilia was excited she could barely contain her emotions. Heck, why should she? She called her mother to share the good news. As her mother answered the phone, before she could even say hello all she could hear was Cecilia's voice on the other end of the line screaming, "I got it! I got it! I got my next artist signed! This means my job is secure Ma!" Cecilia barely even took a breath between words.

"Congratulations Baby! I am so proud of you," Mrs. Bajon said. "Please be sure to work out your contract with the label and make sure your interests are protected." She added a little motherly advice.

"I have Ma. They offered me ten percent of the profit margin on sales of the album if my artist blows up to platinum status or more," Cecilia beamed.

After chatting for a few more minutes about any and everything, Cecilia and Mrs. Bajon said their good-byes and agreed to talk again soon.

It was almost unreal, the way Cecilia took the reins of the artist and guided him from being a local act, to a polished professional solo artist. It was an amazing sight to see. The solo artist Vybe went from wearing off-the-rack outfits to haute couture. He had custom-made jewelry pieces featuring his logo encrusted with diamonds. Cecilia hired one of the best choreographers and stage trainers in the game. If Vybe was going to get to the platinum status that she envisioned, she knew she had to call on the best of the best. When it came time to hire a vocal trainer, she went to a highly sought after professional artist development company. Vybe was ready. His first video had been recorded and was slated for release within a week on BET and MTV. The first single chosen was their song entitled, "Can't Get Enough," a ballad so beautiful and melodic. It can be compared to Kenny Latimore's song, "For You."

Three weeks after the release of "Can't Get Enough," it hit number one on the Billboard Top 100 singles chart. The self-titled album Vybe made it to number five on the Billboard Top 100 Album chart. He was a hit!

To view "Can't Get Enough" Video Scan

The media attention surrounding the solo artist Vybe was crazy to say the least. Everyone wanted a piece of him. Who was this solo artist that appeared out of nowhere, taking the world by storm? Who was the mastermind behind the writing and production scenes?

Girls were rioting at his concerts and extra security had to be hired. He had to use decoy vehicles to move from one venue to the next. It was all surreal.

The entire venture had developed to be bigger than anyone involved had ever imagined. Being the front person for the project, K.K. was challenged in many ways; from the administering of the publishing, to the managerial responsibilities of a highly sought after new recording artist.

In the midst of all the pandemonium, K.K. decided it was time to sit down and catch Rolex up on everything. They met up at the very ritzy steak house, Park 75 in Atlanta. K.K. brought Rolex up to date on all business, endorsement offers, and offers for publishing deals that had already started coming in.

K.K. went on to inform Rolex that ITunes was carrying the Vybe single "Can't Get Enough," and that CDBaby was the online distributor.

"Spineum informed me that they decided to go with CDBaby as their online distributor," said K.K.

"Why did Spineum choose them?" asked Rolex. "What do they offer as a distributor," he continued.

"They set the music up with the other online retailers that will be carrying the single, "Can't Get Enough". They also collect your money from the online retailers, and make disbursements of royalties to Spineum," replied K.K.

"That sounds like a very good set up, sounds like Spineum made a good choice with them," said Rolex.

The last bit of business K.K. needed to discuss with Rolex concerned merchandising. It was time for them to start building the Vybe brand. After closing out that discussion Rolex asked K.K. in a by the way tone, "So how's Cecilia?"

K.K. bursts out laughing in the five star restaurant as he replied, "Man! Did you hear anything I just told you? Have you paid attention to anything I said concerning Vybe," joked K.K.

"Cecilia is doing great though. She is doing a remarkable job with Vybe. I saw her in New York last week. She was saying how much she personally loves the song, and made a statement to the fact of how she could only wish a man would ever feel that way about her," said K.K.

"She does," exclaimed Rolex! They laughed, finished their dinners, and toasted to the beginning of the next things to come.

The name Cecilia Bajon was listed among the "Who's Who?" of the music industry. Vybe's album went platinum in the U.S., gold in Japan, and Sound Scan reported double platinum sales in the U.K.! The frenzy surrounding Vybe was ridiculous, the likes of which had not been seen since the Beetles.

Rolex hosted a small get together at his house in honor of Teno. He invited a few close friends. They ate, drank, and talked about the solo artist Vybe. They even discussed Rolex and K.K.'s intricate plan, and how they had managed to pull it off thus far. K.K.'s account of how everything went down had everyone cracking up!

Cecilia hosted a dinner for Vybe while he was on tour. She made sure that some of the label executives were present. Cecilia viewed the dinner as an opportunity to present Vybe with his platinum sales awards. He was surprised and some of the guest even stood up to speak their well wishes to him. Dom flowed like water, as everyone toasted to the success of the album and partied.

In the midst of all of the festivities, Cecilia decided to check her voicemail because her cell phone had been vibrating all night. She dialed in to the voice messaging system which indicated that she had five messages. The first was from her mother checking to make sure that her baby was doing ok out on the road.

The next message was from Monét, "Girl I am listening to "Can't Get Enough" on the radio and I swear I am about to cry! I love this song! Vybe is the bomb! Call me when you get this message," she hung up. The next two messages were from the label. Her boss congratulated Cecilia on her success with the group.

"Congrats Ms. Bajon, you really found a gem this time! Vybe is taking off even quicker than we expected. I know you all are probably celebrating, and it's well deserved. Call the office when you can, and have fun, but not too much fun!"He joked.

The next message had come in an hour after that one and it was also from her boss. "Cecilia, the festivities may have begun a bit prematurely. I need you back here in Atlanta for a meeting tomorrow morning." His tone had changed drastically from his previous message. She knew he meant business.

Cecilia hung up the phone without even bothering to check the last message in her voicemail box. She grabbed her purse, and whispered in the ear of the road manager. "I'm headed back to Atlanta. Keep things straight here and I will keep you posted on the next move."

He shook his head in the affirmative, and Cecilia left the celebration without another word. Less than two hours later, she was on a plane headed back to Atlanta. She stared out of the window as she racked her brain to figure out what in the world could have caused her boss's demeanor to change so drastically in less than one hour. She was sure that she had crossed all her "T's" and dotted all of her "I's". She had no idea what she would be walking into first thing in the morning when she walked into the label.

After a sleepless night Cecilia walked into her meeting at the label to find that someone had filed a cease and desist order on the album. What could be worse than a court ordered action to stop sales, marketing, promoting, and airplay for the album? With the entire buzz going on about the album and Vybe, this action was sure to draw negative publicity to the solo artist. That was the last thing they needed to happen. The cease and desist had been filed by a former manager claiming that he still had rights to the artist. Apparently, Vybe signed a deal with this manager four years ago. Assuming the contract was dead, he never mentioned it. The contract was only a two year contract . Understandably, Vybe thought the term had ended. As it turns out, the manager slipped four one-year clauses in the contract, which in actuality, made the total term of the contract six years. There wasn't much that could be done at this point, aside from paying the former manager what he was asking in order to withdraw the order.

The greedy manager wanted fifty percent of all earnings. Cecilia, the record execs, and probably even the former manager knew that that was not happening. All parties had to sit down to negotiate a fair and equitable solution to this looming problem. The label was able to settle out of court with the two bit manager for a little more than $450,000.00. This was nowhere near fifty percent of the profits, but enough to make him shut up and withdraw the cease and desist order. Negotiations began and ended so quickly that the momentum behind Vybe never suffered what could have been a major setback.

Anthony Johnson
Business for Pleasure

Chapter 6

"The Smell of Bajon"

F resh dressed like a million bucks, K.K. was rocking' the fresh Sean Jean 2 piece black velour sweat suit, crisp white Sean Jean T-shirt, a pair of fresh white Air Force Ones, and a flat brimmed all black baseball cap slightly cocked to the side. Playing it like the playas play, K.K. had one sleeve pulled up just enough to let the Rolex pop! To top off his fly presentation, K.K. was wearing the cologne that Rolex had custom made while he was visiting France. The cologne was called "Liquid Sex."

K.K. had plans to hook up with Monét tonight. He was on his way to pick her up from the shop where she was going to get dressed after her last client.

When K.K. arrived at the shop the front door was locked, and the reception desk was empty. He figured that Monét must be in the back getting all dolled up for their date. He rang the door bell and was buzzed in immediately. Monét must have seen him on the security camera.

"Hey Hey Hey," K.K. announced his entrance. Monét emerged from the back of the salon with a hot comb in her hand wearing her work smock.

"Hey yourself," she smiled.

"Ahhhhh I see, you're going for the no frills, but still beautiful look tonight. I like it, I like it..." K.K. teased.

"Boy you're so silly! My last client showed up late so I am running a little behind schedule. You can relax and have a seat up here in the lobby, help yourself to some snacks. I'm going to finish up with my client, freshen up, and then we can roll."

An hour passed. K.K. was getting restless. After all, how many snacks can one eat? He called out, "Monét how much longer are you going to be?"

"Just a few more minutes babe," she replied in a sweet sing-song voice.

"You said that an hour ago," K.K. mimicked her voice.

"I know, but I just got a little caught up," Monét said.

"I know you got caught up, in the neckline of her hair I bet! When I came in and saw her I said, "DAMN, it going to be at least two hours, but now we are past that! What's up?" K.K. shrugged his shoulders.

Monét could not hold back her laughter. She laughed so hard she could barely breathe. Between gasps for air she managed to respond "I know, just give me a little while longer." She managed to regain her composure as she stared at K.K. and in her sexiest voice she said "Trust, I'll make it worth your while."

"Now, when you say you'll make it worth my while, you mean like you'll try to give me a few dollars for some gas money, or do you mean that you got a big wet kiss for me, and you're going to let me in to your apartment when I act like I got to use your bathroom after our date?"

Monét laughed again. "Be quiet K.K. I've got a client in my chair right now." She started to make her way back to her workstation, stopped and turned around to look at K.K. "Oh and I'm going to let you in alright." She disappeared again to tend to her client.

Another hour passed before Monét had finished with her client, got dressed, and was ready to for a night out with K.K. She emerged from the back looking like a million bucks in her skinny jeans hugging every curve just right. Her silk blouse was cut just low enough to leave a little bit to the imagination and her strappy stiletto sandals showed off her perfectly manicured toes. Monét walked right up to K.K., wrapped her arms around his waist and kissed him on his neck. "I'm sorry Boo," she purred.

"Oooh that's my spot girl, you better stop playing or we may not make it out the door," K.K. replied.

"Boy you are crazy!" Monét laughed. She looked him in the eyes and asked, "What cologne is that you're wearing Baby? You smell so good!"

"That's Liquid Sex Baby," K.K. replied. "Mmmmm you smell good!" Monét sniffed K.K.'s neck again. A sly grin formed across K.K.'s face.

"How good do I smell," he asked as he wrapped his arms around Monét.

"Let's just say you smell good enough to turn that Liquid Sex into a solid if you know what I mean!" Monét intensified her flirtation with K.K. She couldn't help it, K.K. was turning her on.

"Hell yeah I know what you mean," K.K. exclaimed! It had gotten late so they decided to just head on over to Monét's place to chill out together.

From the way his cologne affected Monét, she was all over him on the way home. She was kissing and touching on him at stop signs, at red lights, even in traffic. K.K. could barely keep the car in his lane.

"Girl I'm going to snatch you out of this car and drag your ass in the woods like a wild wolf, if you don't calm down," said K.K. "Just wait till we get to your house baby! I'm going to rip the brown off that ass baby, your booty gone look like it got vital ago, "said K.K. jokingly.

As K.K. and Monét arrived at Monét's home he couldn't wait to enter the front door. He was ready, sex was in the air. As she unlocked the door, she looked back at K.K., and asked very softly with a very sexy stare in her eyes, "Are you ready for desert baby?"

K.K. responded, "Hell yeah!"

"Do you like cherries baby?"

He responded, "Don't like nothing better!"

"If I feed it to you, do you promise to clean the plate big daddy?"

"I'll lick it cleaner than a dishwasher!"

Monét turned around, threw the door open then yelled, "GOOD!... MOM! K.K. wants some of your cherry pie you made last night."

Monét's mother was babysitting Gerod for her. They burst out laughing! Then Monét turned to K.K. and jokingly said, "That's what you get for being nasty!"

They sat down to a nice movie and spent some good innocent quality time together.

The next day, Rolex was sitting in his kitchen eating breakfast. K.K. walked in cheesing from ear to ear.

"You know your boy almost got Big Daddy status with Monét" K.K. gloated.

"Word?" Rolex chuckled at his boy, walking around with his chest stuck out like he was the man.

K.K. opened the cabinet and grabbed a box of Fruit Loops. "But yo! That cologne is a fool!" said K.K.

"Yeah," Rolex responded, "The ladies love that Liquid Sex."

"To hell with Liquid Sex, that shit should be called Liquid Dick! My neck almost got the panties!" K.K. exclaimed. "Naw but for real, I don't even know if I would have got that kind of play if I didn't have that shit on man. Rolex, you got to let me get a bottle. Please man. This cologne has changed a brother's life! It's like I'm pushing a Bentley when I'm wearing that shit" K.K. joked.

Rolex cracked up laughing. "Yeah I'll get you a bottle man."

"See!" K.K. shook his head. "You should have worn that cologne back when you went to see Cecilia. If you had, she'd be in here right now in one of your t-shirts frying eggs and bacon!"

Rolex continued laughing at his crazy friend, although K.K. may have had a point.

"Do they make this for women?" K.K. asked.

"I suppose they could make it for anyone. It's not like it's off the shelf or anything. I actually sat down with fragrance experts and created that scent last year when I was in France," Rolex explained. "I have a scent custom made every time I travel over there. I've done four so far. After the scent is created and bottled, then you name it whatever you want."

K.K. thought about what Rolex told him as he crunched on his Fruit Loops. "Man, I'm going to make me some shit called Five Minutes Till the Movie Starts, or Gimme Dat Ass, or What Do You Think I'm Doing?, or Coochie in a Bottle, or ...."

"OK! I get the point" Rolex cut K.K. off before he could go any further on his tangent. "Man if I made a fragrance and named it after her, she'd rape my skinny ass! You should make one for Cecilia."

Immediately, after the words fell from his lips K.K. stopped chewing. Rolex also stopped in his tracks. They looked at each other.

"Are you thinking what I'm thinking," asked K.K.

"I think so," Rolex replied. They dapped each other up and started smiling.

Without delay, Rolex got on the phone and contacted the Parisian company that developed Liquid Sex and the other personalized fragrances that Rolex owned. He spoke directly with the fragrance experts to let them know that he wanted to create a feminine fragrance. Rolex explained that the fragrance should be sensual, spicy, with a hint of floral for sweetness. The fragrance experts agreed to send three to four sample fragrances using the elements that Rolex specified. To add to his list of specifications, Rolex insisted that each sample come labeled with the name Bajon.

It took only one week for the samples to come in. As Rolex opened the package he called out to K.K.

"Man come check out these samples and let me know what you think."

K.K. smelled the first fragrance. "Damn! That's real nice" he said. "Oh shit!" he exclaimed as he smelled fragrance number two

"That is sexy." He lifted bottle number three to his nose. He didn't say anything at first. He picked up the other two fragrances and smelled them again. He went back to fragrance number three and pointed to it "Man that's it right there. This shit smells so good I want to take it upstairs and……."

"That's the same one I picked. Rolex took sample number three out of K.K.'s hand and smelled it again. It is so soft and sweet. It's everything that I asked for and then some. Cecilia is going to love it!"

"How are we going to get the perfume to Cecilia," K.K. asked. "What happens if she wants a bigger bottle of it?"

"I'm two steps ahead of you dog. I had Phil Ransom's 800 number printed on each of the samples. When Cecilia calls the number trying to place an order for more, she'll really be calling Phil's office. That's how we'll know that she likes it," Rolex beamed. He was confident that his plan would work perfectly.

"That's all well and good," K.K. added, "but you still haven't told me just how we're supposed to get the sample to her in the first place."

Rolex had an answer for that too. "I was thinking maybe you can meet up with Cecilia at one of Vybe's concerts and drop it in her bag or something slick like that."

"I could do that," K.K. replied "I'll meet up with her and figure something out."

Anthony Johnson
Business for Pleasure

Chapter 7

"When the Music Stops"

K.K. picked up the phone to call Monét. He was out of town with Vybe, and was hoping that she would want to hook up with the tour next week when they were in Atlanta.

"Hey baby girl, its Big Daddy. You miss me yet?" K.K. tried to sound like he was the man.

Monét played right into it. "Yeah I miss you Daddy. When are you coming back to town?"

"The tour is coming to Atlanta next week. I was calling you to find out if you want to hook up while I'm home."

Monét was excited about seeing K.K. She missed his crazy butt. "Oh we can definitely make that happen." She didn't beat around the bush.

They planned a dinner date and then they would go to the concert. K.K. worked out an arrangement with the record company so that Monét would also have backstage access passes. While the tour was in town K.K. would also meet up with Cecilia.

On the night of the show, K.K. picked up Monét from her house. K.K. really wanted to make the night special for Monét. He also wanted to impress her. He made dinner reservations at The Sundial Restaurant, which was located at the top of the Westin Peachtree Hotel. Monét was thoroughly impressed by the beautiful revolving restaurant that boasted one of the most beautiful aerial views of the city of Atlanta. The food and service were impeccable. K.K. could not have made a better choice.

After dinner they made their way to the fabulous Fox Theater. As they made their way through the crowds, lights were flashing, the scene was hot, and the crowd was ready to see their hometown solo artist perform. It was a proud moment for Atlanta to welcome home one of their own.

K.K. and Monét made their way backstage displaying their all access VIP passes. They saw Vybe doing his warm up vocal exercises.

K.K. spotted a familiar face from the label and stopped him to ask. "Hey man, have you seen Cecilia?"

"Yeah man, she's right over there." The man gestured to one of the back rooms with a closed door.

The look on his face raised a red flag with K.K. The dude made a face that clearly indicated that there was drama on the other side of the door.

"What the hell is going on?" K.K. wanted an explanation.

"I don't know," the man replied. "All I can tell you is what I saw go down about twenty minutes ago."

"Come with it then," K.K. pressed.

The man didn't hesitate to give K.K. all of the details. "Man, I was back there with the stage crew checking the last minute details when Cecilia comes storming through here cursing like a mad woman. I mean, she was cussing out everybody from the V.P. to the A&R

folks. Everyone was trying to calm her down so she wouldn't create a scene, but that did not help. The best that they could do was to persuade her into that room back there to curse them out in private!"

A few short moments after the man from the label laid out his version of the story to K.K., Cecilia came busting out of the room. Apparently, she had not lost momentum because she was still going strong, cussing out everyone in sight.

The last thing she said before storming out toward the exit was, "I'M DONE!"

K.K. told Monét to go catch Cecilia and stay with her while he went over to speak with the executives. He was determined to get to the bottom of the matter.

K.K. spoke directly to the VP and asked "Hey, what is the matter with Cecilia?"

The VP shook his head as he said, "You know how it is K.K. When the figures come in, everyone always has a different expectation of what is due to them." He was obviously shaken by his recent encounter with Cecilia.

K.K. yelled after him. "Well I control 50% of all the publishing on this album and I expect to fuck somebody up if I don't get mine!"

The V.P. stopped and slowly turned around. "K.K. this has nothing to do with publishing. It's more label business than anything."

"So basically you are not going to talk to me about what is going on with Cecilia?"

"Right now we just have to keep company business within the company, that's all."

Before heading out to catch up with Monét and Cecilia, K.K. made sure that he dapped up Vybe and wished him luck. K.K.

exited the same door that he saw Cecilia and Monét head out of. The exit brought him to the front of the Fox Theater where he saw Monét trying to comfort her best friend. He couldn't imagine what transpired between she and the record executives that had her so emotionally distraught. As he walked up to them, Cecilia was explaining to Monét that the label was supposed to give her 10% of what the project brings in as profit. To date, they have moved over 7 million in certified sales, with no percentage of returns by the distributors. This meant that, out of about $50 million made there had to be at least $30 million in profit. The record company claimed that Cecilia's calculations were incorrect and that they had realized on $10 million in profit, decreasing Cecilia's share from $3 million to $1 million.

"I'm so tired of going through this!" Cecilia shook her head. "I've experienced this with every single label that I have worked for. I blow up their artists. Then, when it is time to pay me for my services, there is always some obstacle to contend with. The hurtful part about it is that I really thought it would be different with this label, because of the fact that I have a more structured contract. It doesn't even matter though. Especially after their tax attorneys get through deducting every possible expense they can conjure up!"

"Well, what are you going to do?" K.K. asked.

"I'm done K.K. I am absolutely done! I will find something that, for one, pays me based on my worth. Secondly, pays me up front before I break my neck for them." I'll pursue this in court at some point, but for now, I am going to take the money and go!"

It was at that moment that the valet drove up in Cecilia's car. She was so preoccupied with her thoughts she didn't even think to say goodbye to her friends before she hopped in her ride and sped off.

K.K. pulled Monét into his arms as they stood there in front of the Fox Theater. She cried for her best friend Cecilia Bajon. Cecilia worked hard to ensure the success of many artists, and it seemed as if she never received her just due credit.

K.K. reached for his cell phone to call Rolex. Careful not to leave out any detail, K.K. told him about everything that had transpired that evening. Rolex was crazy angry. He was going off so loud on the other end of the phone Monét could almost hear him clearly. K.K. put his hand on his head and pulled the phone away from his ear. He hadn't witnessed Rolex lose his temper this way in years. It made him worry about his boy and what he might do. Rolex was yelling so loud that he couldn't make out everything that he was saying, but he did hear some of the harsh threats that he had made against the Record Executives.

Rolex hung up the phone with K.K. He headed straight to his room and opened a beautiful mahogany jewelry box. He reached in and pulled out a business card, the same card that Cecilia gave to K.K. when they first bumped into each other at the record store. Rolex picked up his phone again and started to dial Cecilia's number.

"What the hell am I doing," Rolex said out loud after the first ring.

Cecilia's soft voice on the other end of the line jolted Rolex back to his senses. He could tell that she had been crying. He wanted to comfort her so bad, but if he revealed himself right now, the plan would be ruined. He hung up the phone and fell into a deep sorrow for her. "I'm so sorry baby," he said softly into the air.

The night air seemed to have lost its cool breeze as Rolex moved through the house in stealth mode. His persona was deadly and his attitude was without mercy. He navigated to a safe that sat in the back of a closet, punched in the digital code, and it opened. He retrieved a small black phone book from the safe, grabbed the phone, and dialed the number.

Whoever Rolex called was obviously the right person for what he had on his mind at that time. About an hour went by as Rolex made calculated moves throughout his home. Then, the door bell rang. When Rolex answered the door, there stood one of the hardest looking gangsters the city had ever witnessed.

Rolex simply made eye contact with the man at the door. Without words, Rolex grabbed his bag from the floor, and jumped in the back seat of the black SUV the visitor was driving. As they pulled out of Rolex's driveway, it was revealed that the SUV Rolex was riding in was actually the lead vehicle of a three vehicle convoy of all black SUV's. The SUV's disappeared into the night at a very high rate of speed. They arrived at a private airport on the west side of Atlanta about an hour later. There were two private jets on the tar mat awaiting the arrival of Rolex and his crew. There were a total of fourteen men with Rolex at the private airport. This was just a small fraction of his old crew when he was still living the life.

Rolex finally spoke. "I need five of you in New York tonight!" He tossed them an envelope. "In this envelope you will find an address and instructions for what you are to do once you arrive!" Five men boarded one of the available jets. The jet immediately hit the runway and took off for New York. He continued, "I need five of you on this jet. There's a mansion that sits on 120 acres of land in Austin, Texas. I want the porch light of that house shining on your fucking shoes in three hours!" Rolex tossed them an envelope just as he did the first crew. They boarded the awaiting jet. It also took off immediately, headed for Texas.

Rolex and four other men jumped back into the black SUV and sped off into the night. About four hours later, Rolex and his crew appeared out of nowhere at the Alpharetta home of renowned bachelor and CEO of Spineum Entertainment. They hit that house like a bull dozer during demolition. They snatched him out of bed, and took him to a well lit area of the house.

"Listen to me you greedy mother fucker! Tonight you're going to pay Cecilia Bajon or the undertaker, your choice," said Rolex. "You will cut a check for $2 million dollars to Ms. Bajon for her part in the success of your artist, Vybe!

"I'm not writing shit," the CEO yelled! "What you gone do kill me? Then do it then Mother fucker," he continued.

Rolex spoke very calmly as he said these next words to the CEO. "I've got a better idea than that. I know there are only two things that matter to you. One being your sister and the other being your parents."

Rolex handed Spineum's CEO his cell phone and told him to call his sister's home. The CEO started crying as he dialed his sister's phone number. The phone rang twice before one of the men Rolex sent to New York answered her phone.

"Stop crying mother fucker and call your parents," shouted Rolex. He dialed his parent's phone number in Texas, and one of Rolex's men answered the phone there as well. "Now what the fuck you gone do," asked an angry Rolex.

"Ok! Ok! I'll pay her, I'll pay," shouted the terrified CEO. "Please don't hurt my family," he begged. "Please don't hurt them!" He wrote Cecilia Bajon a check for $2 million dollars and handed it to Rolex.

"If this check don't cash that's your ass," said Rolex as they exited the home.

Nothing was ever said about Rolex's visit to Spineum's CEO. No one was hurt in any way. However, it was very clear that Cecilia Bajon was not to be messed with. Cecilia received her settlement check from Spineum Entertainment by courier at her home the next day.

The Vybe project had brought Rolex over $10 million in earnings to date. His lawyer, Phil Ransom, made sure that all monies had been collected. All monies included: publishing royalty money from album and single sales for foreign and domestic, mechanical royalty money from airplay, licensing money, and last but not least, ring tones, and all downloads. Rolex made about 1.3 million on ringtones alone. The project proved to be an extremely profitable venture for Rolex. Rolex did look out for his boy K.K. He cut him a check for $2 million. Rolex put the other $8 million in an investment to be paid out quarterly for years to come.

A few weeks after the ordeal with Cecilia and Spineum Entertainment Group, Cecilia officially resigned.

It was extremely difficult for Cecilia to spend her days lounging at home with nothing to do. She was accustomed to making power moves and calling the shots. Sitting at home watching Maury had zero appeal. The highlight of her day was when she made her daily call to Monét. They talked about everything from fashion, to finances, to relationships...mainly Monét and K.K.'s. Monét filled Cecilia in on

K.K.'s antics in trying to win her affection. He could make her laugh so hard she wanted to cry, even during the worst of times. Cecilia was really tickled by Monét and K.K.'s silly love affair.

Wishing she had a man to comfort her during this trying time, she really regretted the fact that she had neglected her personal life for so many years. To make matters worse, at the end of the day, the one thing she did love and focus all her energies toward showed her no love. She did miss her solo artist Vybe very much. She walked over to her CD player and popped in his CD. It was almost like she had never heard the songs before. She started really listening to the lyrics that Rolex wrote especially for her. She started to cry, her heart yearned for a man to love her so true. *Maybe one day I will be so lucky*, she thought. As she took a long introspective look at her life, she started to think differently about her priorities as it pertained to her career, personal relationships, etc... It was like a new woman had emerged out of the pain that had tormented her spirit over the past few weeks. Cecilia was ready to take chances, ready to explore new possibilities.

Anthony Johnson
Business for Pleasure

Chapter 8

"A second chance"

K.K. looked at himself in the rearview mirror as he was driving home after leaving the barbershop. His barber had really hooked him up. His low fade was tight. At that moment he heard his boy Vybe crooning, "Can't Get Enough" over the airwaves. He was instantly reminded of his and Cecilia's last conversation before she left the record label. He started to think how perfect it would be to get Cecilia to endorse the perfume that Rolex had created for her. He changed his course and drove straight over to Rolex's crib so that they could devise yet another perfect plan!

He and Rolex sat down to fine tune the details of K.K.'s idea.

"Since you already have an 800 number set up with Phil Ransom, we can actually establish a company, a perfume company," said K.K.

Rolex liked the sound of that. He shook his head and said, "I can contact the company that created the fragrance and find out what it would take to mass produce the scent they made for Cecilia. Then we will pay her to be the spokesperson for the fragrance. A huge endorsement deal will rejuvenate her career. It's perfect!"

Rolex immediately got on the phone with Phil Ransom to explain the details to him. Phil got busy with setting up the company, and making contact with the fragrance experts. All of the legal business behind a venture of this magnitude was going to take some time to sort through. Rolex used part of the $8 million that he made off of the success of Vybe project as the budget for the perfume company. It took all of three months to complete, but finally everything was in place. The company was ready to introduce its new perfume by the name of "Bajon."

No one would know that K.K. and Rolex were behind this venture, because fortunately they had Phil Ransom in position as the front man. It was a perfect plan. As a means to raise public awareness about the perfume, the company put on promotional campaigns, commercials, billboards, magazine ads, etc. The perfume was being marketed like any perfume manufacturer would market a fragrance. The only difference was that they had not introduced a spokesperson.

Unknown to Monét, K.K. had started to leave samples of Bajon in the beauty salon.

Everyone, including Monét, loved the scent.
Soon, as Rolex and K.K. had planned, Cecilia
heard about the new scent. She too fell in love
with it. She didn't know who manufactured it.
However, she knew they were right on point for
naming it Bajon because she felt like it was
tailor made for her!

Finally, the time had come for the
perfume company to approach Cecilia Bajon
and ask her to endorse their fragrance. While at
home one day doing laundry, and some light
housekeeping, Cecilia heard a knock at her
door. She opened the door, and in front of her
stood a courier with a medium-sized package.
Without a thought, she signed for the package,
thanked the courier, and closed the door behind
him. She brought the package over to the
couch for further inspection. She took the top
off to reveal its contents. She was absolutely
shocked! There was a huge bottle of her now
favorite scent, Bajon. There was a card and

letter attached. She quickly tore open the card and it read:

Please accept this custom bottle of our new perfume Bajon as a special gift to you...

Reading the card further intensified her curiosity about the contents of the letter. She opened it and read the letter:

Dear Ms. Bajon,

Our Company is aware of your extremely impressive career in the entertainment industry. We had the pleasure of reading the featured article about you in the publication, "Who's Who in Entertainment." It is with great pleasure that we extend the invitation to you to join our team and become the paid spokes model for our premier fragrance.

We hope that you will accept this invitation because a fragrance as beautiful as Bajon can only be represented by one as beautiful as you (the fact that our perfume bears your name can only serve as an advantage in our marketing strategy). We thank you in advance for considering our proposal. Please contact Phil Ransom at 1-800-555-5557 to discuss further details.

Cecilia sat on her couch, absolutely motionless staring at the letter she just read. She thought surely she had to be dreaming. This could not be real. She read the letter over and over, at least five times, as if to further check its authenticity. Her mind was having a hard time grasping the concept of someone asking her to be a spokesperson, a model. *I'm no model!* She thought to herself. Cecilia was flooded with all kinds of emotions at that moment. As she tried to collect herself, she remembered how she had told K.K. and Monét that she was looking to do something that paid up front. This offer, if it was in fact legitimate, was absolutely amazing. It was almost, too good to be true. What were the odds that her new favorite fragrance would not only bear her name, but that the manufacturer would ask her to endorse a product that she felt was made especially for her? Uncanny to say the least!

Once the levity of the situation sank in, Cecilia was ecstatic! She screamed out in excitement, "Thank you Lord! Thank you!" as she ran around her house. What she felt at that very moment could only be described as joy. She grabbed the telephone and dialed her best friend. She didn't even wait for Monét to answer the phone before she started screaming. Monét went into panic mode. She recognized Cecilia's voice on the line, but could not make out a word she said for all of the screaming.

"Hello! Hello Cecilia! Are you ok?" She spoke with intense concern.

Cecilia calmed down long enough to say, "Monét I am ok. I am more than ok!" She explained the whole turn of events to Monét and once again she started her screaming tirade. This time Monét joined in. Her excitement matched Cecilia's. Somehow they understood every word the other one said.

Finally Monét asked, "What are you going to do Cecilia?"

"I don't know," Cecilia replied "I guess I'll start by calling the number they provided in the letter to get more information. I just don't know what to say, what questions to ask."

"I know one question you need to ask...how much does the job pay?" Monét was only half-joking. "But for real girl you need to call these people and find out what they are talking about in the way of compensation. If the money is right, everything else can be worked out," she added. "The rules are: you ain't giving up no ass, and you ain't doing no gay shit! If you do, I will call yo' momma and daddy. You know they will have yo' ass collecting tithes on Sunday morning, and printing gospel newsletters for the rest of your life. They may even stick your ass out there on Old National Hwy with a bucket that says, "THE OAK BAPTIST CHURCH," Monét joked. "Naw, but in all seriousness, don't be ackin' all brand new when you blow up. I'm still doing your hair! Get all fancy if you want to, I'll burn your shit out!" Monét was on a roll. They both cracked up.

Monét could not have been happier for her best friend.

"Cecilia you were just saying how you wanted to do something different. This could be it girl, give it a shot. It looks like these people know what they are doing. Obviously they have done their homework. They know who you are, what you do, where to find you, etc."

"You're right Monét. It just all seems too good to be true."

"Don't talk it down," said Monét. "Check it out first before you start in with all the suspicions. All I can say is, you have an angel looking out for you girl. That angel saved your job at the label, and now you're presented with this wonderful opportunity. We need to go out and celebrate tomorrow night!"

"That sounds great! I need to get out of this house anyway. I am starting to drive myself crazy with nothing to do day in and day out," Cecilia laughed. "Lord knows I need to get out and have some fun."

"Meet me at the shop at about 9:00 p.m. I should be finished with my last client by then," said Monét.

"Ok," agreed Cecilia.

"And girl, please wear something that says, I'm single and classy, not I'm Catholic and celibate!" They laughed some more and then ended the call.

Monét called K.K. to relay Cecilia's good news.

"Well check that shit out!" said K.K. "Shawty finna blow up! Mariah Scary, Anita Faker! What is Cecilia's little chicken leg ass gonna do to sell some perfume," he joked. "Man, that's alright. I am really happy for her. I know she's gonna accept the offer right," K.K. asked Monét .

"Yeah, I think she will."

"I'm about to call Cecilia myself!"

"Alright," Monét said warily, knowing how much K.K. liked to tease, "Just don't give her a hard time about it."

"I ain't," he promised.

Cecilia's phone rang, and K.K.'s voice was on the other end. He immediately started in on her, "Look at your old Martha Stewart of music, Lil Kim's auntie, can't cook because your daddy thought you wouldn't go to college ass! Congratulations girl!"

"K.K. shut up, you nut!" Cecilia laughed so hard her stomach hurt!

"So when are you going to sign," K.K. asked. He was trying to get a first hand sense of Cecilia's feelings toward the offer.

"I don't know," Cecilia answered sounding unsure. "I need to learn more of what this is all about."

"It's about time to get paid," said K.K. "What you need to do is tell them you want $500,000.00 up front. Plus, you want a 10 percent stake in the company." K.K. went on, "50 Cent got that kind of deal with vitamin water."

"They are not going to give an unknown like me a deal like that," Cecilia thought K.K. sounded crazy.

"Well, how are you going to know until you ask," he challenged. "Who are you? Ms. Cleo? Call me now!" joked K.K. "Naw, but for real, at least ask for it. If they want you bad enough they will be willing to pay. But one thing I know is, you ain't giving up no ass, and you ain't doing no gay shit! I will call your Rev. Al Sharpton acting daddy, and I bet he'll have your ass singing Christmas carols in front of Wal-Mart with a mission pin on your jacket!"

"Boy you are so silly. Get off of my phone!" Cecilia laughed at how much K.K. and Monét were starting to sound alike.

"Just do it girl. You are drop dead gorgeous Cecilia. These people know what they're getting. You would look so pretty in the ads and TV commercials. You're the perfect person for it, plus, it's your last name! Could it be any more perfect," K.K. urged.

"K.K. you sure are pushing mighty hard for me to do this." Cecilia observed out loud.

He realized that he did come on kind of strong, and he didn't want to blow his and Rolex's cover. He joked, "Hell yeah, because when you blow up, I'm going to be right there with you, banging all your model friends!"

"Oh I am telling Monét," Cecilia playfully threatened. "Bye boy," she said and hung up the phone.

She could hear K.K. still pleading on the line saying, "You can tell them I am your little brother..."

Monét and K.K. were very happy for Cecilia and her good news. After all that was said during their conversations; the most valuable bit of advice Monét offered was when she told Cecilia to talk it over with her mother first.

Cecilia's mother was a retired educator. She retired from Clark Atlanta University in 2005, as a Black History professor. She was not a lawyer and wouldn't offer much on the lines of legal advice. However, being a highly intelligent woman, surely, she would help Cecilia put things in prospective.

As she talked with her mother, Cecilia had many concerns. One concern being if she should take an opportunity at something she had no clue of. Her mother said to her in a very soft tone, "An opportunity is just that, an opportunity. Let me tell you a story," said her mother. "When I was a little girl I always dreamed being a nurse. There wasn't a lot of opportunity for it, especially for a young black woman in the south. I filled out applications for several nursing programs, and never got a response from any of them. I would call the schools to check on my application. Most of them couldn't even locate my papers. After being turned down or pushed away whenever I called, I decided to go back down to one of the schools in person. When I arrived at the front desk, I told the receptionist that I was there to check on my application for their nursing program. She told me the program was full. As I began to walk out of the office, the receptionist called me back to her desk. She told me they had an education program that she could put me in immediately. I took the opportunity as fast as I could. I didn't know anything about the education program, but I knew I wasn't going to turn it down. I found out what it was about, and earned one of the first master's degrees handed to a black woman from that school.

"Grab this opportunity child," said Mrs. Bajon softly. "Find out what you need to know. Then be the best they've ever seen. Do it. Don't run from it, learn it."

As Cecilia and her mother talked, they shared some homemade cookies just like they did when Cecilia was a little girl. While they talked, her father quietly walked in the kitchen, grabbed a few cookies, and spoke into air. "There's always room for you at the church." Cecilia and her mother laughed at her father's comment. They wrapped up their conversation. Cecilia kissed her parents and headed home.

After discussing this once in a life time proposal with her mother, Cecilia was ready to negotiate with the perfume company. She assembled a team of lawyers, managers, and accountants. Cecilia contacted the perfume company by way of her legal representation. They negotiated on her behalf, everything from percentage structures to branding deals. Cecilia was set. She landed a very good contract to endorse the Bajon perfume line.

It was obvious that Cecilia had learned her lessons in business. She continued to struggle emotionally from the way she was treated by the record label. With a new career to focus on, Cecilia was definitely on her way to healing. Two weeks later, Cecilia accepted a staggering $1.1 Million advancement. She also received a thirteen percent stake in the Bajon Perfume Company, as the new spokesperson. For the next six months, Cecilia lived, slept, ate, and breathed Bajon perfume. Advertisements were popping up everywhere: T.V., magazines, billboards, etc... Everywhere you went you were bound to see a picture of Cecilia Bajon's beautiful face. Not only was Bajon a great product, but the marketing team behind the fragrance had truly struck a nerve with consumers. The company quickly soared to the top of the fragrance industry having grossed upwards of $52 million in sales. Cecilia had no trouble collecting her monies from the perfume company. Rolex saw to it that Cecilia was well compensated for her work, and then some. Her bonuses were nothing to shake a stick at.

◊ ◊ ◊

Anthony Johnson
Business for Pleasure

Chapter 9

"Straight from the heart"

The next day, K.K. was over Monét's house while she was getting ready to go to work. He watched her go through about five different outfit changes, and countless shoes to take with her to work. She and Cecilia planned to paint the town red! K.K. approached Monét with the suggestion of him watching her son while she hung out.

Monét immediately dismissed his offer stating, "I don't let everybody keep Gerod."

K.K. took her statement personally and replied, "I'm not just everybody." Monét realized how offensive her statement must have sounded and started to explain.

She couldn't even get a word out before K.K. interrupted, "No! You listen to me now. I understand that you have to be careful at all times when it comes to your son. I don't take it lightly either. There are risks involved with entrusting the care of your child to someone. Just realize that I am not just everybody. I care for Gerod. When I come to your home to visit you, I'm just as anxious to see him and to find out how his day went as well. You have to understand that I would never harm a hair on his head, or allow anyone else to. Monét I've always accepted you as a package deal. I've never thought of you and not included him. When I call you in the morning to make sure you made it to the shop safely, I also ask you if Gerod got off to school ok. It's because I care."

For once K.K. was as serious as a heart attack. Tears rolled down K.K.'s face as he continued. "I've never had a father in my life. All my mother and I have ever had was each other. The day my mother died, I felt that this world would be unkind to me from that point on. I've held on to senseless things over the years, trying to find happiness. All I ever found was another opportunity for a letdown. It is not easy being alone, with nothing to hold on to but memories. Memories are fine, but they damn sure can't hold you back. When I met you Monét, I felt like God was pleased with me. I felt like the world had been kind to me. From the first day I saw you at the mall, I could feel my blood boil. Warm sensations came over me, and lead me to you. I realized that I was crazy about you from the first time we kissed. I knew I was in love with you when you turned and walked away afterwards. I feel a void when you're not around. I look at Gerod like he is my son. I hope that one day he will be. All I want to do is care for both of you, to make sure that nothing but happiness enters your lives."

Monét started to cry, unable to speak. She kissed K.K. and held him for a long time. She realized that she had been so used to being the protector of her home that she sometimes tended to be over protective. It was never a matter of her not trusting K.K. He had been fabulous with both her and Gerod. He never gave her a reason not to trust him. What she said earlier was simply out of fear. She didn't mean to hurt K.K.'s feelings.

When they ended their embrace, she picked up the telephone and called her mother to tell her that she didn't have to watch Gerod that night, and that K.K. would be coming by to get Gerod for the evening. He was going to stay at home with K.K. while she and Cecilia went out. She hung up the phone. She and K.K. embraced once again staring into each other's eyes with a new understanding.

K.K. phoned Rolex later that day. "Man, I think she's going to do it," he said before even saying, "Hello."

Rolex knew immediately who and what K.K. was talking about. "She is excited!" Rolex smiled at the thought of his and K.K.'s plan coming together.

"Man, excited is an understatement. Word of this perfume is spreading like wildfire. The demand for this stuff is like crazy. Who in their right mind wouldn't want a piece of something like that?" K.K. answered.

Rolex believed in striking while the iron was hot. He decided to reach out to Phil Ransom to ask him to set up a meeting immediately concerning the endorsement offer.

Later on that evening Cecilia pulled up in front of Monét's shop as planned. When she stepped out of the car, she heard some guy's cat calling at her from across the street.

Normally, it would annoy Cecilia when guys acted so immature, but she knew she looked smoking' hot in her fitted black satin corset dress. Her thick black curls hung heavy to one side of her head framing her perfectly made up face. Tonight she felt as bold and beautiful as she looked. Her bright red lipstick was the perfect tie-in to her 4 ½ inch red bottom stilettos. She truly looked like Hollywood royalty. Instead of giving them the snub, she graciously turned around, waved, and said a quick "hello." When she turned back to go into the shop, Monét was standing there with the door open grabbing for her arm.

"Girl you better get your Lola Falana, Grace Kelly, Dorothy Dandridge looking ass in this shop before one of them men try to steal you!"

Monét locked the front door before they walked to the back of the shop. Monét was still going on about Cecilia's look. "I see you finally listened to a sistah, that outfit DEFINITELY has class written all over it!"

Cecilia folded her arms and tapped her foot as she examined Monét in her black baby tee, skinny jeans, and flip flops.

"I wish I could say the same about you. Why do I always have to wait for you to get ready Monét? Shoot! I am ready to go out," complained Cecilia.

"Girl hush! It's not going to take me any time to get ready. My last client wanted me to take her from Buckwheat to Beyoncé!" Monét clowned as she made her way to her office to freshen up and change clothes.

Cecilia cracked up laughing and asked, "Did you work that miracle girl?"

Monét answered, "Honey, I had her looking at least as good as Cheryl Cross-eyed, but that's the best I could do. I'm a beautician, not a magician." Then she disappeared behind her office door.

"Hurry up," Cecilia yelled as she laughed and spun around in one of the salon chairs.

Twenty minutes later Monét emerged from the office looking like a star in her own right. Her one shoulder magenta mini dress hugged her ample curves in all of the right places. Her feet were dressed in sexy 4 inch Manolo Blahnick sandals. Her short pixie cut was perfectly coiffed, and her make-up was flawless.

"That's what I'm talking about girl." Cecilia got up from her chair and walked over to Monét for a closer inspection. "You sure you don't have a magic wand up in there?" Cecilia gestured toward the office.

"Oh so now you got jokes!" Monét smiled at herself in the mirror as she pushed a few wayward strands of hair back into place.

Monét and Cecilia left the shop and hopped in Cecilia's car. The venue for tonight was a place called the Piano Bar. The Piano Bar was a ritzy spot located right in the heart of Buckhead, where the Who's Who of Atlanta liked to gather to enjoy live jazz music and see who's who.

On the way to the club Monét asked Cecilia, "What is the real reason why you haven't dated in so long? What happened after college when you left ATL," asked Monét.

"What do you mean," Cecilia asked, immediately feeling defensive.

Sensing her friend's uneasiness, Monét softened her tone "Girl when we were in college all you talked about was finding the man of your dreams once you left Georgia. I know your dad has always looked at relationships as the devil's plan to throw you off of your path, but you're grown now girl. You are a woman and you need a man. What gives?"

Cecilia's countenance became heavy. Her friend was right. Initially she shied away from relationships to please her dad, but now as a grown woman her reasons for remaining single were more of a personal choice. She wasn't sure that she wanted to live the rest of her life based on that choice that she made long ago. Cecilia wanted to be happy. She wanted to let go of her past. She wanted to love. She decided right then and there that the first step to moving forward with her new lease on life was to share a bit of her past with her best friend.

Cecilia swore Monét to secrecy. "What I am about to tell you girl, I want you to take it to the grave. Do you promise?"

"I promise!" Monét couldn't imagine what Cecilia had to tell her that was so serious, but she reassured her. "I will not tell anyone your business, not even K.K."

Cecilia began to recount her painful past. "When I left town I had no experience with men and relationships. I was a virgin, and extremely naïve. I met this guy in California. From what I could tell, he was a single and eligible fitness instructor. We used to go out. He showed me around L.A. He took me to all the hot spots and helped me find my way around. We spent practically all of our time together. I believed him when he told me he loved me. I gave him my virginity. He was gentle." Tears started to well up in Cecilia's eyes. Her voice started to crack. She had no idea how much pain she still felt behind this. She became so overwhelmed with sadness that she had to pull the car over.

Baffled, Monét reached in the glove compartment and pulled out a tissue to give to Cecilia. Cecilia wiped her face and continued her story.

"He was gentle. He treated me like I was the most delicate jewel, like I was precious to him. The next day he sent me roses and a card that said, "You gave me your flower, so here is mine to you..." I was in love.

Three weeks later I started getting sick to my stomach every day. I later found out that I was pregnant. I told him the same night that I found out because I was so scared. I didn't want to be alone in it. I needed him to comfort me. Instead, he told me that it was easy to keep a pretty woman a secret. He was a Fitness Instructor, and all of his clients were pretty women. However, it would be impossible to keep a baby a secret from his wife.

Monét could not believe her ears, but she dare not interrupt Cecilia while she told her story.

Cecilia continued, "He told me that he was sorry before he started beating me."

Monét's eyes grew wider and wider the more Cecilia spoke.

"That damn man beat me until he knew that the baby was dead. He almost beat me until I was dead. I didn't die obviously, but I did pass out. The neighbors heard all of the commotion and they called the police. I woke up in Cedar Sinai Hospital six days later with a broken pelvis and in critical condition. The baby was gone, and so was my womb. They had to do an emergency hysterectomy."

Monét reached out and hugged her friend. Monét cried just as hard as she held on tight to Cecilia. They cried for awhile.

"I love you Cecilia. It breaks my heart to hear that happened to you." Monét cried even harder.

"I love you too girl. I can't help but to wonder sometimes am I worthless as a woman? I mean, I am actually scared to date because I'll have to face the truth. Rather than to deal with that, I immersed myself in my career. People seem to accept that as a legitimate excuse for my not having children. Monét this man didn't just try to take my life. He took my baby's life. He took my daddy's dream of becoming a grandfather." Cecilia shook her head.

"Yes you are a woman. A beautiful, strong woman and my prayer for you is that you find a man that loves you whether you can give him children or not. I also pray that God will show his mercy and grace upon your life." Monét spoke from the heart. "Cecilia, we've been friends since grade school. I always felt very close to you. When you just spoke to me about what happened to you in California, I felt closer to you than I ever have. Thank you for talking to me my sister. You just gave me the courage to open up about a very bad time in my life also," said Monét. "I've been hiding the truth from everyone about me and Jay, Gerod's dad, and how we busted up."

A very puzzled Cecilia asked, "What do you mean? We all knew you caught him with the stripper chick! What else happened Monét? Did he have a child with her or something?"

"No," said a very emotional Monét. "No! It was so much worse than that!" Monét began to cry so hard that she couldn't catch her breath long enough to speak.

After wiping the tears from their eyes and pulling themselves together, Cecilia shouted out, "What the hell did he do?" They both busted out laughing. After a good laugh Monét began to speak.

"Jay was part of a social group that met up on Tuesday nights to play poker. They had a specific place they played, and never changed location. I used to ask him why he never brought any of his friends around, but he just brushed me off. He told me everyone was always busy. I didn't press him about it after that, but I never forgot that he refused to engage me with the topic either. Well one day while at the salon, Jay called to see if I wanted to go to lunch. I said, "Sure." I told him to come pick me up. He showed up around 12:30 p.m., and that's when it happened!"

"What girl," shouted Cecilia, totally drawn in to the suspense of the story.

Jay walked into the salon to pick me up and Corey yells out,"Hey Jay," said Monét.

"Who is Corey," asked Cecilia.

"Corey was a flaming gay stylist I rented a booth to. My heart stopped! I thought I would die," Monét sadly explained. Well needless to say I followed him to the poker game that next Tuesday."

"No Monét! No!.. Don't tell me this girl," Cecilia angrily shouted! "No more," shouted Cecilia. "You don't have to say it girl I understand! I just want you to know deep down in your heart that his actions had nothing to do with you. You don't lack anything, you are all woman. Any straight man will be lucky to have you. I say this to you because some women try to blame themselves, or question if they were not enough for a man." Cecilia explained.

"I know girl!" said Monét.

The two distraught women held each other and cried. They shed years of hurt and pain. Betrayal ran down their faces. As they cried their wounds started to heal. By sharing their stories, Cecilia and Monét were able to help one another move forward from their past. After a little more crying, the ladies pulled themselves together once again. They never made it to the club that night.

Monét returned home only to find K.K. and Gerod asleep on her living room sofa. Seemed they decided to just stay there and watch movies. The empty fast food packages, popcorn bags, and soda bottles were evidence of a great evening for the guys.

Monét picked up Gerod from the sofa. Since he already had his pajamas on, she took him upstairs to his bedroom. Lovingly, she put him in his bed and kissed him goodnight. Of course K.K. waited around for his good night kiss when she came back down stairs as well. Thanks for allowing me to keep Gerod tonight. We had so much fun.

"He made me promise to take him to ride go carts next weekend if it is ok with you," said K.K. They both laughed.

"Thank you baby! You are a good man and I'm sure you'll be a great role model for Gerod," said Monét. They began to kiss. It was so beautiful and real. K.K. gently laid his hand on the side of her face almost to support her head as she leaned into his grasp. She wrapped her arms around that man as to say, "Please don't ever leave." They kissed more as they embraced each other tighter. Nothing else mattered at that moment. They were trapped inside of an emotion only the two of them could understand. She pulled him down to her sofa, as she submitted her herself to him. She took his hands and placed them in places that haven't been touched since she left her ex. They were very in tune with each other's erotic side as they began to slowly undress each other. Knowing where this was headed, K.K. still made sure to respect the woman he was so in love with.

He whispered in her ear, "Are you sure baby?"

"Yes K.K....yes! I'm yours baby!"

Unable to make it to the bedroom, they began to make passionate love right there on her sofa! He kissed her and licked her in places that made her scream! She returned every favor as she treated him like her favorite flavored lollipop. They made love for hours as they explored to find each other's pleasure points. She straddled him like a cowgirl, as she rode herself to a climatic explosion that they both experienced at the same time. It was beautiful, gentle, sticky, and as fulfilling as either had ever indulged in. They laid there staring and smiling at each other, as they tried to catch their breath. They were simply unable to move for awhile.

After about an hour of lying there, they assured each other that what just happened was mutual. The moment was enjoyed by both of them. They kissed and decided to call it a night. K.K. gathered his things together and headed home shortly after.

After straightening up her house, Monét turned all the lights out and retired to her bedroom. As she walked past her bed, she saw a note on the night stand accompanied by a Touchy Notes greeting card.

The note read; *Monét, thank you for understanding me, and allowing me to be a part of you and Gerod's life. I feel I'm a part of a family with you two. I know it will take time, but I hope to one day be with you guys forever, as your husband and his step dad. I love you. K.K.*

P.S. Here's a Touchy Note for you, it reads "You Complete Me" signed, K.K. You can get these Touchy Notes greeting cards at www.touchynotes.com if you like them. I think they're real cool to keep in your wallet or purse for that moment's gesture.

Monét smiled and nodded her head in agreement. She loved the card. After a night like she and Cecilia had, she couldn't help but be teary eyed after she read that beautiful note K.K. left on her night stand. Since she had just made beautiful, passionate love to him, it made it mean that much more.

The next day while at the salon, she went to the Touchy Notes website, and bought several packs. She began giving them to her customers when they came in needing a lift. After a few weeks, Touchy Notes became a normal thing around the salon with all the stylists and their clients. Monét and K.K. began presenting them to each other on a regular basis from that point on as well. The slogan is true. They really are "Touchy Notes for Touchy Folks."

Anthony Johnson
Business for Pleasure

Chapter 10

"Advocates for Success"

B ig things were happening all around for Rolex and K.K. In addition to their successful investment with the music and the perfume company, they were working to open a recreation facility in the College Park neighborhood where they grew up. This fully funded facility boasted a state-of-the-art computer lab, full indoor and outdoor basketball courts, a football field, gourmet kitchen, cosmetology classes, auto repair shop, classrooms, and conference rooms. Volunteers and paid professionals were hired to teach the various academics, trades, and sports to the surrounding community.

Rolex and K.K. found themselves spending most of their time over seeing the completion of the recreation facility. Naturally Rolex's real estate development company was tasked with building the 40,500 sq. ft. facility located in the heart of College Park, GA. This was the same place where Rolex ran the streets, sold drugs, guns, and stole cars. As a grown man, he felt a sense of obligation to rehabilitate his community so that the next generation did not have to go down the same negative path that he had.

Rolex got up the next day bright and early. He was happy, felt good, and seemed to have been in a great mood. He had very important business to tend to that day. Unlike the business he would have normally been conducting; Rolex's business was directed at Ms. Jackie, his mother.

After finding Christ, Rolex went to his mother and convinced her to enter into a 12 step program for her alcohol addiction. Convincing his mother to commit to a 12 step program was not an easy task. There were lots of arguing and very heated discussions. Rolex was relentless at his attempts to get his mother the help she needed for her sobriety.

Eventually, Rolex won his mother over. She had agreed to check into the program, and did very well after adapting to her treatment. Ms. Jackie took what she learned during her treatments and shared it with troubled teens at a local center for at risk teens.

The business that was so important that day for Rolex was, his mother was being recognized for completing the 12 step program. K.K. joined Rolex as they celebrated Ms. Jackie's new lease on life.

Proud would've described how Rolex and K.K. felt towards Ms. Jackie as they witnessed the ceremony. Later that evening they offered Ms. Jackie a position to run a program for at risk teens at the new community center they were opening in College Park, Ga. This program would be much like the one she had been volunteering with. She accepted the offer of course, and was eager to get started, once the center opened.

Two weeks before the grand opening, Rolex and K.K. met at Rolex's office at the real estate firm to tie up all loose ends pertaining to the opening.

"I spoke with the Mayor's office today." The Mayor is scheduled to arrive thirty minutes prior to the opening. It is very important that we stay on schedule that day," said Rolex.

"I've secured Vybe for a performance in the auditorium," K.K. added. "The food and beverage companies will make their deliveries two days before the opening."

"Alright, it sounds like everything is pretty much on track. I'll be meeting with the staff tomorrow to make sure that everyone is on the same page with the flow of events," Rolex stated.

K.K. pushed his chair back, stood up from the table, and stretched. It had been a long day of making calls to vendors, meetings, etc.

"Ok, well I am about to get out of here, and hook up with Monét for the rest of the evening," as he reached out to give his boy a pound.

Rolex gave K.K. a pound, but remained seated looking at his notes. He also had a long day. He wished he could head home himself to relax but unfortunately his to-do list had not been completed.

"Alright man, I have to run back over to the facility to finish up a few things with the HVAC Company. Ya'll have fun," he said to K.K.

Being the last person left at the office, Rolex locked up, then jumped in is Ford F-250 Dooley pick-up truck. He headed over to the recreation facility to meet with the HVAC Company. They called him earlier to advise that they would be late due to issues with the heat zoning. There were so many thoughts racing through Rolex's mind that the twenty minute ride from the office to the recreation facility seemed more like two minutes. Rolex could not understand why he was feeling so uneasy at that moment. The best he could do was chalk it up to wanting everything to run smoothly at the opening. Besides, he had so much on his plate. He arrived to find that the HVAC people were not at the site. He reached for his cell phone and called his contact at the HVAC Company. They told him that the crew had already come and gone. They dispatched the crew to go back over to the site which would take about thirty minutes.

Rolex decided to wait there in his truck instead of rescheduling the appointment. With only two weeks left until the opening, a matter as important as this could not be put on hold, not even one more day. As he looked out at the beautiful facility that sat in front of him, Rolex thanked the Lord for how far he had brought him from his past. Although there was nothing that he could do to erase the awful things that he had done as a youth, he vowed right then and there to make a positive impact on the community from that point on. He had to laugh to himself when he thought about how much of his energies these days were focused on improving the lives of others. It was a far cry from the Rolex of the past. He thanked the Lord yet again.

K.K. headed straight to Monét's shop to pick her up after leaving his and Rolex's meeting.

Monét kissed K.K. on the cheek as she got into his car "Hey baby, I'm hungry can we go get something to eat before we head to the house," she asked.

"Yup," K.K. said as he merged into traffic.

"I spoke to Cecilia today. She said that she's homesick and wants to come home," Monét said in a matter-of-fact tone.

"Call her and put her on speaker." K.K. wanted to check on her himself. Monét dialed Cecilia's number on her cell phone and activated the speakerphone. "Hello," Cecilia answered.

"Hey girl, I know we just spoke a few minutes ago, but I have someone with me that wants to speak to you. I have you on speakerphone."

K.K. took that as his opportunity to jump in the conversation. "What up Toni Wackston, Feclia Keyes, why don't you bring your little homesick ass home?" he exclaimed.

"Shut up boy!" Cecilia dismissed K.K.'s comments, and moved on to another topic of conversation "What are ya'll up to," she asked.

"I'm finna take Monét's hungry ass to the butcher to buy half of a cow," K.K. joked.

Monét playfully punched him in the arm. "Shut up K.K., you are so silly," she giggled.

"Naw you shut up with them fake Capri pants on," he responded to Monét, but quickly turned his conversation back to Cecilia.

"Cecilia, Monét got on some high waters trying to pass them off as capris! Come to think of it, it looks like she got on a pair of Gerod's pants!" Monét and Cecilia busted out laughing at that fool K.K.

K.K. got a kick out of making the girls laugh so he continued on. "Cecilia, you need to stop laughing so hard because I saw that picture of you at the class picnic. You better hope that shit don't leak out on the internet cause your image consultant would be on your ass if he saw that hairpiece you let Monét glue to your head. That shit looked like a damn squirrel in handcuffs being lynched with a bungee cord!"

Cecilia and Monét laughed so hard that tears came streaming out of their eyes. They remembered exactly what K.K. was talking about, and his observations were only slightly exaggerated.

"Ok we're at the butcher shop we'll hit you back later," K.K. said.

Cecilia was still trying to gain her composure when she answered, "Ok, ya'll.

Monét I'll call you later on tonight. I need to talk to you about something."

Monét said, "Ok." Then, they ended the call.

Anthony Johnson
Business for Pleasure

Chapter 11

"Confessions of the Heart"

After grabbing a bite to eat, K.K. and Monét went straight to Monét 's house. They were lounging on the couch watching television. An emergency news break interrupted the program they were watching. K.K. jumped up from the couch immediately when he recognized footage from the news cast at the recreation facility they just built. Police lights flashing and part of the property was sectioned off with crime scene tape. K.K.'s mouth hung open as he listened to the reporter say that there had been a double shooting at the newly constructed recreation center in College Park, GA. The camera panned the area and stopped on Rolex's bullet riddled Ford F-250 pickup truck. All that K.K. could make out were bullet holes in the windshield and driver's side door. K.K. fell to his knees and hollered "NO! NO! NO!!!"

Monét immediately rushed to his side. She tried to put her arms around him as she asked, "What is it baby? Tell me what's wrong," she screamed! Her heart was beating a mile a minute.

The reporter indicated that two men had been shot only moments ago. One man was an unidentified HVAC contractor. The other man, whose name was unreleased, was believed to be the person responsible for erecting the facility. A motive had not yet been confirmed. The police believed that it may have been an attempted robbery for the spools of copper for the HVAC system.

"Damn Rolex," K.K. said to no one in particular as he jumped to his feet, grabbed his keys, and was out the door.

Monét was right on his heels. It was a good thing that Gerod had stayed over his grandmother's house that evening. They rushed straight over to Grady Memorial Hospital. K.K. hadn't seen the inside of Grady hospital since long before his mother died. On the way to the hospital, K.K. told Monét everything that he and Rolex had been keeping from her and Cecilia. Starting from the day that Rolex visited Cecilia at her office, the solo artist Vybe, down to the perfume company, he told her every single detail.

"You could have been honest with me," Monét said to K.K. in a comforting voice. She stared out of the window while trying to let all of this new information process in her head.

"I believe that," he replied. "There was just too much riding on the confidentiality of this thing. I had to keep it under wraps, for Rolex. Baby that man loves Cecilia! All of this has been his way of taking care of her," K.K. shared.

It was at that moment that everything started to make sense to Monét.

"Rolex is the angel," she mumbled to herself as she burst into tears. "Oh my God! I can't believe this is happening right now!" she shook her head.

"Baby," K.K. reached for her hand. "Are you angry with me? Are you gonna stay with me or leave me Monét," he asked.

She looked him in the eyes and said, "K.K. you are my Boo. I am with you for life! Now let's go on up and see about Rolex. We're alright," she assured him.

They prayed the rest of the way to the hospital that Rolex was ok. K.K. was totally overcome with fear. His cell phone started blowing up! Phil Ransom was the first to call. He was also hysterical.

"What happened man? Is Rolex ok? Are you with him? I'll meet you at the hospital!"

Phil didn't even wait for an answer before he was in his car on the way to Grady. Teno was the next to call. He also said that he would meet K.K. at the hospital. The next call came from Vybe. Then, one by one each member of Vybe's crew called K.K. They wanted to find out where Rolex was so they could rush to his side as well. People from all of Rolex's ventures and company were calling K.K. Monét took K.K.'s phone and started to answer the calls because she knew he had too much on his mind with the uncertainty of Rolex's condition.

Rolex was in surgery and the doctors couldn't provide much information at that point. The waiting room was crowded with people there to see about Rolex. The pain that each of these people shared in their hearts for Rolex was a mere testimony of the work that God was doing in and through Rolex's life. Rolex had touched so many people. They prayed that God would show his mercy on Rolex, and spare his life.

Divine intervention is the only thing that could describe the fact that Cecilia's desire to come home became so overwhelming that as soon as she ended her telephone conversation with K.K. and Monét, she booked a flight online. Within an hour and a half, she was on a plane headed back to Atlanta. Her plane was scheduled to land in twenty minutes. No one knew that she had actually decided to come home, let alone that she had made the arrangements so quickly. A voice inside of her told her that she should leave right then. It could only have been God that prompted K.K. to call Cecilia when he did, and it was God that told her to come home.

Upon touching down in Atlanta, Cecilia called Monét. The phone rang and rang until finally it went to voicemail. Cecilia called again, same thing. No answer. She must have left at least five messages letting Monét know that she was at the airport. She figured Monét and K.K. might have been "tied-up" at the moment. Therefore, she decided to sit tight and give them a few minutes to handle their business before she called back. She smiled to herself. She had to be sure to let K.K. know that a few minutes was all she gave him credit for! It would serve him right, for all of the jabs he had taken at her and Monét. While she waited at the airport, the television newscast caught her attention. The top story was about a real estate developer that was the victim of a robbery just a few short hours ago. When they posted Rolex's picture on the screen, Cecilia's heart nearly stopped. "Real Estate Developer," Cecilia shouted.

Back at the hospital, the waiting room was filled with Rolex's people. Thank God, he spared Rolex from the grips of death that night. He did, however, take two bullets to the stomach and one to the shoulder. Although he wasn't completely out of the woods, the worst of it was over.

The thought occurred to K.K. that Cecilia deserved to know what was going on behind the scenes for so long. The events of the day only confirmed that life is too short and tomorrow is not guaranteed. He was going to tell Cecilia everything. He told Monét that he intended to do so. "If she hates me for it, then so be it." He could live with that. What bothered him more was the thought of his boy almost having lost his life and never having the opportunity to be with his one true love.

He was convinced that Cecilia would come around if she truly understood how pure Rolex's heart was for her.

Monét wiped the tears that fell from KK's eyes. She squeezed him as a sign of assurance that she was there for him. She kissed him on the cheek and told him that she was going to call Cecilia right then. She pulled her cell phone out of her purse and went out into the hall to place the call. When she looked at her phone she saw that she had five voice messages from Cecilia. She retrieved the messages only to find out that Cecilia was already in Atlanta at that very moment. She didn't walk, but ran back into the waiting room to tell K.K. the news.

"Cecilia is home! She's back in Atlanta!"

K.K.'s eyes were wide like saucers as he listened to what Monét was saying.

"She is at the airport. I am going to go get her," Monét said as she held her hand out for K.K.'s car keys. He handed them to her without a second thought.

"Be careful baby. I'm going to stay back here and hopefully they will let me in to see Rolex."

K.K. and Monét shared a quick kiss on the lips and Monét was out the door.

Monét called Cecilia as soon as she got in the car.

"Monét what's going on?" Cecilia inquired. "I called you like five times. I need you to pick me up from the airport."

"I'm already on my way." Monét replied.

"Where the heck have you been? I mean, I know I popped in on you and everything, but I did tell you to expect my call tonight," Cecilia teased, giving Monét a hard time for making her wait at the airport.

"I'll be there in twenty minutes. I'm coming from Grady Hospital," Monét answered.

Cecilia was immediately concerned. "Grady? What's wrong? Is Gerod ok?"

"Gerod is fine... Its Rolex," said Monét.

"Rolex," Cecilia inquired. "Why in the world are you at the hospital with him? I did see something about him on the news just now. Was he involved in some sort of shooting? Monét, did I tell you he had the audacity to come to my office awhile back? I'm getting really nervous right now. Monét, what do you have to do with Rolex?" Cecilia was perplexed.

"Look, Cecilia, calm down, I will be there in a few minutes and I will explain everything." Monét tried her best to sound calm when she was actually feeling quite to the contrary. With that they ended their phone call.

Less than twenty minutes later, Monét pulled up in front of the terminal where Cecilia was waiting for her curbside. Cecilia got in the car without a word and just looked at Monét as if for an explanation. Monét stared straight ahead with both hands on the steering wheel.

"Cecilia, I found your angel," Monét said as she pulled away from the curb and into the flow of traffic.

"Monét what in the hell are you talking about," inquired Cecilia. She was getting sick of all of the cryptic talk. She wanted straight answers.

"Remember not too long ago when we were discussing all of the events that had transpired in your life over the past year or so. I made the comment that you must have an angel looking out for you." Monét tried to refresh Cecilia's memory.

"Yes, I remember!" She was growing impatient.

"Cecilia what I'm saying is that all of those things are not arbitrary." Tears began to well up in Monét's eyes.

Cecilia sat quietly, listening intently, trying to imagine what in the world Monét could be talking about.

"There is a man. There is a man whose love for you Cecilia is pure and true..."

"What are you saying Monét?" Cecilia shouted.

"It's Rolex Cecilia! Rolex is in love with you!" Monét went on to explain everything that K.K. had explained to her just an hour or so earlier. Cecilia was absolutely dumbfounded and totally at a loss for words.

Monét added, "Rolex and K.K. have been behind all of the major events in your life over the past year and a half. When you ran into K.K. at the record store that day, he went home and told Rolex he saw you. That is how Rolex knew your whereabouts. K.K. is the only person that knew anything about Rolex's feelings for you. When you rejected Rolex that day he came to your office, it didn't discourage him one bit from still trying to take care of you and wanting to see you happy."

"I accidentally mentioned to K.K. about you being in jeopardy of losing your job at the record company. Rolex and K.K. used their resources to have the album done so that Vybe would become a success and more over, so that you could keep your job. Cecilia the lyrics to those songs were written by Rolex about you. It was all for you, so that you would be ok. All the business was conducted under K.K.'s government name Kendall Jackson. Remember when the label shitted on you and cheated you out of your money causing you to quit? Rolex called a company in Paris to have them create a fragrance specifically for you. Bajon is that perfume. The whole name thing was no coincidence. The perfume was made just for you. You were the only person who could have possibly been the spokesperson. Do you hear what I'm saying? It was Rolex that put that $1.1 million in your pocket! If all that ain't love, I don't know what is."

Both women were crying at this point. Monét cried because she sincerely hoped that her friend would not let her fears hinder her from experiencing the love that she deserved. Cecilia cried because she never imagined that anyone could be so concerned with her well being. She was embarrassed by how she behaved when he came to her office that day. She knew that she had dealt with him way too harshly. She didn't understand why she treated him the way she did. There was something about him that scared her. It was the attraction between them. It was strong. She didn't want to succumb to it. Not with a bad boy like she believed Rolex was.

Monét's voice interrupted her thoughts. "K.K. is afraid that you'll be pissed at him. Rolex has always felt like you would hate him even more if you were to ever find out."

"I don't know what to say," Cecilia uttered softly. "You mean to tell me that all of the lyrics in those songs expressed Rolex's feelings toward me? Those were some of the most beautiful words that a man could ever say to a woman." Her words trailed off.

"Yeah, and he said them to you," added Monét.

"Cecilia, I know you have your preconceived ideas of who you think Rolex is, but Rolex is a Christian man now. K.K. got him to get out of the game years ago. He accepted Jesus Christ as his Lord and Savior. It has been his desire to do nothing but good ever since. Rolex took his money and started a real estate development firm. The place where Rolex was shot tonight was the recreation facility that he and K.K. built for the College Park community. K.K. told me you are the one that can complete Rolex's life! Now that is a heavy statement. I am sure that he is just repeating what Rolex told him."

They rode in silence for the rest of the trip. Monét figured she had given Cecilia enough information to digest.

To Cecilia's surprise, Vybe's hit song; "Can't Get Enough" came on the radio. Cecilia listened to the song like never before. She let the words penetrate her heart. A small voice inside of her said, "Lives can change."

"Don't judge the man for what the boy did," Monét pleaded.

"I won't anymore! Monét, get me to him," she exclaimed.

"You got it!" Monét was more than happy to oblige.

Cecilia and Monét arrived at Grady and rushed into the waiting area of the hospital. K.K. stood to his feet when he saw them enter the waiting room. Cecilia walked over to him and hugged him tightly.

After they embraced, she took a step back, looked him in the eye and said "K.K., thank you! Thank you so much! I know about everything that you and Rolex did for me!

"Thank you." K.K. grinned sheepishly. "You mean you're not mad?"

"I am the furthest thing from mad. I am grateful," she hugged him again. "How is Rolex?" asked Cecilia. She was extremely concerned.

"He just came out of surgery. The doctor said that the surgery was successful, but his condition is still critical!" K.K. looked like he had the weight of the world on his shoulders. It was easy to see that Rolex and K.K. were more than just boys, they were brothers.

"Do you think I can go in and see him," asked Cecilia.

"Yeah, they said that he can have one visitor and only for a short time. I haven't allowed anyone in to see him. You go ahead." He gave Cecilia his approval.

Cecilia quietly entered the room where Rolex laid in the bed with IV's in his arm. She pulled a chair up to his bed and spoke softly to him.

"Hello Rolex, this is Cecilia. First, I would like to thank you for all the wonderful things that you have done for me. You made so many of my dreams come true. Secondly..." her voice cracked, "I want to tell you that I am so very sorry for the way that I treated you. I was really ugly to you that day in my office. I am so ashamed that I judged you so harshly. Truth is, you've been my angel." Cecilia cried like a baby for the second time that day. "I realize that it could have only been God that sent you to me."

"When I was a little girl, my mother bought me a musical box. It had a beautiful ballerina that danced when you wound it up and the music began to play. It was so pretty to watch. I would watch the ballerina twirl, but the true beauty was when I closed my eyes and listened to the music. Rolex, you are that music to me now. The day you came to my office I thought you were so fine!" She managed a laugh. "I recognized you right away. I couldn't forget that face. It scared me that I was as attracted to you standing there as a grown woman, as I had been as a young girl in high school watching you walk up and down the halls like you were King Tut. I am saying this to say, Rolex; I would like to be there for you this time. I want to be the one to help nurse you back to health. I want to be there for you now, and, for as long as we can be." She grabbed his hand and held it. For the slightest moment Cecilia felt Rolex attempt to tighten his grip on her hand in confirmation. It was as if GOD had tapped Rolex on the shoulder and said, "Wake up." After he heard the beautiful tone of Cecilia's voice, Rolex's eyes had opened gently. You could see the hint of a smile as it crept across his lips.

"Shhh! Please don't try to talk Rolex," said Cecilia. Rolex did not adhere to that command. For the first time in his life he would have been granted the opportunity to confess his love to Cecilia face to face. Only death could have stopped him from doing so.

With his finger he gestured for Cecilia to come closer, so that he could say something to her. As her beautiful face came closer, his body began to shiver, as though a cool winter breeze had blown over him.

Rolex stared into Cecilia eyes for few seconds then he softly whispered, "I love you Cecilia, and I always have. I want you in my life so I can love you. I want to take long walks in the park with you. I want to hold your purse while you're shopping baby. I want you to brag on me to all your girlfriends of how happy I always make you. I'll cook great meals to feed you. I'll hire designers to dress you baby. Cecilia wiped Rolex's cheek as a single tear escaped from the duct of his eye. Please baby, just give me a shot at loving you girl," said Rolex. "Let me be the man I was made to be to you. I'll carry your burdens on my shoulders Cecilia. Life is yours to live now. Please baby share it with me."

As the tears ran down Cecilia's face, she stopped Rolex from speaking and said to him..."I'm yours if you'll have me." She smiled as she leaned down and gently sealed it with a kiss.

Two months later, the biggest grand opening in the history of College Park, GA took place. The College Park Recreation and Vocational Center was officially open to the public. It was a very festive event. Rolex and

Cecilia were there together. K.K., Monét and Gerod held hands family style. Phil Ransom was there with his wife along with all of Rolex and K.K.'s friends and family. They were all there to celebrate the welcomed addition to the city of College Park, Ga. The addition was a beacon of hope to the lives of the youth.

The newscast that evening featured a wonderful story of the opening. It was great to finally see some positivity highlighted in the College Park community. Just as quickly as one could let the warm and fuzzy feeling sink in from the new beacon of hope in the heart of College Park, GA; the news transitioned to national news. One report in particular was a story out of California about a popular personal trainer to the stars.

The trainer was the victim of a brutal home invasion. The report stated that an unknown group of men invaded the Los Angeles home that the trainer shared with his wife.

Although a motive had not yet been determined, police believe the attack was personal. The invaders did not steal anything from the home, nor did they harm anyone else living in the house. Only the trainer was beaten severely, and is now in a coma at Cedar Sinai Hospital. He also suffered severe and permanent injuries to his genitalia, forever banishing his chances of reproducing.

The End

Anthony Johnson
Business for Pleasure

I Love You Rolex...Cecilia

Author's Note

At this time I will allow you to imagine what love is to them. Put yourself in Cecilia's shoes and love, like you know she will love Rolex. Then, put yourself in Rolex's shoes be genuine and love truly, like you know he will love Cecilia. Then maybe you'll see that your *ANGEL* is right there next to you!

Thank you for reading "Business for Pleasure."

Sincerely,

Anthony Johnson

K.K. And Monét continued to exchange TouchyNotes. To view all of the TouchyNotes catalogs, visit www.touchynotes.com.

JUST
THINKING
ABOUT YOU

LOVE *Monet*

YOU'RE
ALWAYS
ON MY MIND

ALWAYS *K.K.*

www.touchynotes.com

Create your own your Touchy Note!

LOVE_____

www.touchynotes.com

Poems by Rolex to Cecilia...

Where You at C?

*I ran those thousand miles.
I climbed that tall ass mountain.
I swam across that sea, and still didn't find
my baby!*

*I yelled to the top of my voice.
I sang a bit sweeter than a hummingbird.
My calls all went unanswered, and I still
couldn't find my baby!*

Rolex

Don't wake me

A woman like you
A jewel uncut
8th wonder of the world

A scent so sweet
Skin so smooth
Hair with big black curls

You walk on clouds
Make pulses dance
Get in a man's spirit

Eyes that pierce
Voice so soft
It was a dream,
but I can still hear it

Rolex

Good Morning

If I could wake and find you here laying next to me

I'd serve you breakfast still in bed with coffee or hot tea

I'd bathe you in the warmest bath then slowly rinse you off

Lotion you down and moisturize you to make sure you stay perfectly soft

I'd patiently help you pick out your clothes and match the right pair of shoes

I'd treat you like a bullion of gold because our lives would be perfectly in tune

Rolex

Loving You

I spend all my days loving you from afar,
Admiring you like a bright shining star.

Who wouldn't with all your splendor?
But unlike the others, I can love you tender.

Caressing your life with the finer things,
To you, joy is what I want to bring.

Making you have butterflies at my sight,
While knowing each day, I can love you
right.

Rolex

So Many Ways

I am just a man with a million wishes.

One, to hold you close and steal a thousand kisses.

Sit and massage your feet a hundred times.

Please baby know that I don't mind.

To say I love you in so many ways.

Not just one but 365 days.

Rolex

You're So..

When I think of your smile it warms me inside
The tone of your voice is electric

It makes me feel I can conquer the world
Not having your love is hectic

I need you to love, other women won't do
I desire your warm embrace

I'm just a man that loves everything about you
Your style and your beautiful face.

Rolex

You!

She was sexy
She had class
She spoke with intelligence

She was appreciative
She had desires
She's more driven than most

These are things I always saw whenever I closed
my eyes

The day we met, I knew it was you
Damn! What a surprise.

Rolex

Visions of You

My heart is yours if you want it,
My soul is willing when you need it,
I will provide all that matters,
I will offer an abundance,

Loving you is what I've dreamed of,
Needing you describes my life,
All I own is yours tonight,
All my visions say you're my wife.

Rolex

Dying Wish

If I was given 60 seconds to live, my last request would be, to lay my head on your chest; so I can listen to your heart beat as mines stopped.

I love you Cecilia Bajon!

Rolex

No Shame

I'll pay your bills
Then I'll take you shopping
I'll buy you a home
And won't let you mop it

I'll feed you dinner
Then I'll be desert
I'll break you off
Make you go berserk

I'll buy you cars
You can't even pronounce
Exotic furs
Perfume by the ounce

If I was your man
I'd give you the world
Cecilia Bajon
You need to be my girl!
Rolex

Social Media

To Checkout New Artist and Music from Spineum Entertainment visit us at
www.spineument.com

To View the Touchy Notes greeting cards go to
www.touchynotes.com

To Download the song, "Can't Get Enough" go to
www.itunes.apple.com/us/album/cant-get-enough-ingle/id534527357

www.cdbaby.com/cd/zac1

To View "Cant Get Enough" Video Scan